DOLLY

LORI BEASLEY BRADLEY

Copyright (C) 2018 Lori Beasley Bradley

Layout design and Copyright (C) 2019 by Next Chapter

Published 2019 by Liaison – A Next Chapter Imprint

Edited by Marilyn Wagner

Cover art by Cover Mint

This book is a work of fiction. Names, characters, places, and incidents are the product of the author's imagination or are used fictitiously. Any resemblance to actual events, locales, or persons, living or dead, is purely coincidental.

All rights reserved. No part of this book may be reproduced or transmitted in any form or by any means, electronic or mechanical, including photocopying, recording, or by any information storage and retrieval system, without the author's permission.

I

The late spring heat in the house made the air practically unbreathable.

Dolly jerked her head up from the sewing in her lap when she heard the wagon outside. She set the cloth aside and went to the window to see Karl, the delivery man from Haney's mercantile, jump from the wagon. She went to the door with a smile on her face. He was there with her new wash tubs — the ones with wringers to press the water from the clothes.

"I can only bring this to your front porch, Miss Dolly," the sinewy young man apologized. "I gotta make a run into Holbrook to pick up merchandise for Mr. Haney at the depot or I'd stay to carry it to the back and set 'em up for ya."

Dolly shielded her eyes from the bright sunlight with her chapped hand. "That's all right, Karl. I can get it from here and set them up."

She wasn't sure that was the truth, but Dolly knew she needed to get the crate and its contents off the front porch and to the back before Martin got home and saw it.

Karl slid the large wooden crate from the back of the wagon and carried it to the porch. He stood waiting until Dolly dug into her apron pocket and fished out a nickel. "Thank you," she said and handed the young man the coin.

"Thanks, Miss Dolly," he said as he dropped the nickel into the breast pocket of his worn plaid shirt, "this'll buy me a drink at Bud's when I get to Holbrook."

The driver hurried back through the gate, climbed back onto his wagon, unset the brake, and urged the horses up the dusty street. Dolly stared at the ungainly crate and pondered at how she was going to get it to the back porch where she did her laundry. She grasped onto the rough wood and lifted one end. She lowered it back to the porch, thankful it wasn't too heavy.

"You need some help with that?"

Dolly lifted her head to see her neighbor, Trace Anderson, standing at the gate. Dolly felt her cheeks flush. She'd been sweet on the widowed man for a long while.

"I can probably get it, Trace," Dolly said, "but I really don't want to scratch the floor, dragging it to the back."

Trace opened the gate and walked to the porch. "Where's Martin?"

Dolly rolled her eyes. "Your guess is as good as mine. I have no idea where my brother is today." She pushed open the front door and bent to take hold of one end of the crate. "It's not too heavy."

Trace squatted and picked up the other. "Not too heavy," he said with a warm smile, "just awkward."

Dolly returned the big man's smile. "It's new washtubs with a set of wringers to save my poor hands when I do the laundry."

"It was nice of Martin to do that for you."

"Yah," Dolly said with a soft snort. Her brother hadn't had anything to do with it. Dolly had paid for the tubs with the money she'd saved from the eggs and produce she sold to Mr. Haney.

They hauled the crate through the parlor, careful of the lamps, and through the tidy kitchen, where chicken boiled in a tall pot for dumplings, and out onto the back porch. "If you have a prybar," Trace said, "I'll pull this apart for you."

"In the shed." Dolly stepped off the porch into the yard and went to the little building behind the house connected to her chicken coop. She came back with the iron prybar and handed it to Trace who took it and began wrenching off the thin wooden slats of the crate. "I can do that," Dolly told him, "if you're busy in your shop."

Trace Anderson ran a saddle and tack business attached to his home across the street from Dolly and her brother in Concho, Arizona. He did a good business with the Mormon ranchers and farmers in the area and was well liked in town. Women at church said he was one of the most eligible bachelors in the small community since his wife had passed two years before.

Dolly had set her eye on him some time ago, but the man had never paid her much mind. Ten years her senior, perhaps Trace thought she was too young at twenty-four to be a proper wife and mother.

"It's no bother." He pried the boards off the end of the crate and began to slide out the two tubs mounted on legs, so Dolly wouldn't need to do the laundry on her knees anymore. He lifted out the two rollers and studied them. "What the heck are these?"

"Wringers," she said with a proud smile. "You mount them to the tub, twist that handle there, and feed your clothes through." Dolly shrugged her shoulders. "They wring out most of the water, so it doesn't take so long for the clothes to dry."

"Sure would save a soul's hands some from all that twistin'." He studied the tubs. "Which one you want them on?"

"Makes no never mind," Dolly told him, and Trace began affixing the wringers to one of the galvanized tubs. "Martin would say this was a waste of good money, but it's my hands they are saving and not his," Dolly said with a nervous laugh. "And it was my money I bought them with — not his. Martin will probably say I'm taking the lazy woman's way out of doing the washing."

Trace cleared his throat as he turned his curly, head of brown hair to stare at Dolly. "You shouldn't pay any attention to what Martin says about you, Dolly. I know you work hard to keep Martin's house in order and tend to the garden and the chickens." He stared into her blue eyes with his hazel ones and Dolly couldn't look away. "He's got no call sayin' the things he does to you or sayin' it the way he says it."

Dolly was stunned by the man's words. How could he know what sort of things Martin said to her? She glanced at the cheese cloth over the open kitchen window and sighed.

Martin was a yeller just like their father had been. When he'd been drinking and wanted to make a point, he thought saying it louder would do the job. Trace had lived across the street from them for over ten years, first with his late wife, Lucy, and then alone. How many of Martin's foul-mouthed rages had he heard? Were they the reason he'd never paid any attention to her?

Sudden embarrassment caused Dolly's cheeks to flame and that filled her with anger. She took a deep breath and tried to gather some control of her irritation. "I'm sorry Martin's ranting has disturbed you, Mr. Anderson. I'll be certain to remind him the windows might be open the next time."

Trace, with a frown on his handsome face, tightened the final nut and tested the security by wiggling the wringers with his large hand. "I think that'll do it." He stared at the pile of wooden slats strewn across the porch. He nodded to the mess. "Do you want me to carry those off for you?"

"I'll break them up for the cook stove," Dolly said without looking him in the eye, "but thank you."

She smelled her chicken boiling in the kitchen and stepped around the big man, who towered over Dolly's five feet seven inches by a head and had shoulders, so broad he had to turn them to get through most doors. "I need to check the water in my chicken before it scorches in the pot."

Trace turned his head toward the kitchen door. "It smells good," he said with a grin, "but all your cookin' smells good, Dolly."

Dolly smiled as she lifted the lid from the blue enameled pot. He'd been smelling her cooking? Well, he did live just across the way. Dolly liked to cook and took pride in her meals. She was also proud of her weed-free garden and her plump chickens.

It still riled her some that Trace had been paying so much attention to what was going on at her house when he had never given her more than a nod in passing in public. Dolly knew Trace had never been much of a conversationalist though. Maybe he was more of a listener than a talker. She smiled to herself. The Lord knew she could use someone to listen to her for a change.

Trace stepped into the kitchen. "Well, I guess I'll be goin' if you don't need anything else," he said as his eyes scanned the tidy kitchen, "but remember what I said. Martin's got no reason to call you lazy or treat you the way he does."

Dolly felt her cheeks flush again. "I appreciate that, but Martin has been taking care of me since Mama and Daddy died." She bit at her lip as she pondered what to say next. "He put his life on hold to look after me." She parroted the things Martin always said to her.

Trace snorted. "He treats you like a child and uses you like a house slave, Dolly. You're not that skinny little girl who lost her parents anymore," he huffed, "so have a little pride and stand up for yourself like the grown woman you are now. You've done more than your share to pay that worthless drunkard back."

"I owe my brother for looking after me all these years," she protested, defending her brother with tears stinging her eyes, "and what right have you to listen in on our private family squabbles anyway, Trace Anderson?"

"There isn't much of a way to avoid listening in," Trace smirked, rolling his eyes. When Dolly made no reply he marched out of the kitchen, through the parlor, and out the door.

Dolly let the tears she'd been holding back slide down her cheeks. If he thought she was a woman now, why hadn't he ever paid court to her?

❧

Trace swallowed hard as he stomped across the narrow street separating his house and tack shop from Dolly and Martin's. Why had she gotten so cantankerous? He'd only been trying to help. How was he not supposed to listen to Martin's drunken rampages when the man yelled every word?

He yanked open the front door and stormed inside his house.

He'd been listening to that bastard beat and degrade that girl for ten years. Trace shook his head in frustration as he stomped to the pail of water on the kitchen counter, lifted out the enameled dipper, put it to his lips, and swallowed the cool, sweet water. He hoped it would cool his temper, but it didn't.

Trace returned to the worn canvas settee and dropped his girth down onto it. He picked up the framed tin-type photograph and ran a calloused finger over Lucy's smiling face. "I've done the best I could for that girl, Lucy," he whispered. "I went to Reverend Haskell about Martin beatin' her the way he does, but the old man told me to mind my own business. He said Dolly was Martin's responsibility to raise the way he saw fit. He told me to remember what the Good Book said about sparing the rod and spoiling the child."

Trace returned the photograph to the table. "I even went to Martin about courtin' her after a proper mourning period had passed," he whispered, "but the drunken bastard laughed in my face and told me I couldn't afford his bride-price for her hand." Trace shook his head again. "I know you liked the girl, Lucy and so do I. She's grown into a fine woman." Trace smiled at the photograph of his wife. "I was in her house today and it's so clean I could have eaten off the floor, but she has no respect for herself. Martin's beaten it out of her."

Trace picked up the harness straps he'd been working on before going to assist Dolly and began to stitch them together with a needle and sinew. He couldn't get the pretty blue-eyed redhead across the street out of his head though. He'd watched her grow from a gawky girl into a shapely woman.

He remembered how Dolly had been there for him after Lucy had passed, trying to give birth to their child. She'd wept at the funeral, and then come to the house and taken charge of the kitchen where women from town had brought platters and dishes of food.

Those days had passed in a blur of sadness and tears, but he remembered the skinny young woman in his house, cleaning, making him food, and pressing him to eat. Trace honestly didn't know what he'd have done without her help during that time. He'd asked Dolly to stop coming after he'd overheard some of the women at church remark about the unseemliness of him having the girl in his house so much so soon after the death of his wife.

Trace had suspected they were jealous of Dolly because they hadn't thought to send their eligible daughters to his aid. Later in the conversation, he'd heard one of them remark that she hoped he never set his eyes upon her daughter. The big man had killed poor Lucy, filling her belly with a babe so big it couldn't make its way out and she didn't want to take a chance like that with her poor girl. Filled with grief and guilt, Trace had told Dolly he thought it was time he tried to get along on his own and asked her to stop coming over to clean up after him and do his laundry.

He'd missed her company but thought it best for the both of them. Now years had passed, and Dolly had grown into a beautiful young woman. She had all the qualities a man could want in a wife, but Trace knew her brother had turned every young man in town away when they'd asked to court his pretty sister.

Martin wanted to keep Dolly to himself to tend to his needs as a housekeeper. Was that fair to Dolly? No woman wanted to take the unemployed drunkard, Martin as a husband. He's going to turn her into an old maid, living with and looking after her brother because he's made her feel guilty. Trace had heard the man tell Dolly that no man would ever want to take her as his wife because she was a lazy, worthless human being with the looks of a dried up old cow.

Trace thought back on the day he'd gone to Martin's door and ventured to ask him to court Dolly in the hope he could save her from yet another beating and haranguing.

"What's on your mind today, Anderson?" Martin had said upon answering the door, his breath reeking of alcohol.

"I want to talk to you about Dolly, Martin."

"What about her?" Martin stepped out onto the porch and closed the door behind him. "You finally gonna pay me for all the work she's been doin' for you over there?"

"I'd like to pay court to your sister, Martin."

"Sure you would," Martin had sneered, "and get more of her

services without payin'." The disheveled man had gone to the porch swing and dropped into it. "I'll tell you what I tell all the other horny little cocks who show up here sniffin' after my sister. Meet my price of a hundred dollars in gold and you can have the lazy little cunny."

Trace's mouth had fallen open in surprise and disgust. "You're obscene," he'd spat, "to talk about Dolly like that."

"Why?" Martin had smirked. "It's what you all want—what's between those legs of hers." He'd shrugged. "Meet my price and you can have it, but, like all the rest around here, I doubt you will come up with it."

Trace could have met Martin's price, but he didn't want to think of Dolly as a whore. Men only paid other men for the use of a woman when that woman was a whore and that wasn't Dolly.

2

The new washtubs with their wringer made Dolly's laundry day so much easier.

She stood pinning laundry to the line and looked up to see Trace sitting on his porch with work on his lap. The man was always working. He saw her at the line and nodded.

When Dolly waved, the strong breeze caught the shirt in her hand and tugged it away. She watched in horror as Martin's fancy new dress-shirt tumbled across the dusty yard. She forgot about Trace Anderson and dashed off after the shirt.

Her heart fell when she picked up the wet garment and shook it to dislodge dust and debris. The red dust of the yard stuck to the fabric in several spots. With a deep sigh, Dolly turned to hurry back to the tubs and get the shirt back into the soapy water before stains set.

When she turned, Dolly saw her brother glaring at her from the porch with a cup of coffee in his hand. "Is that my new shirt?" he demanded.

"The wind yanked it out of my hand." Dolly defended as she moved toward the porch. "I just need to rinse it out again."

Martin turned his head to stare at the new washtubs and Dolly waited for the explosion. "What the hell is this?" he demanded. "And where did it come from?"

Dolly stepped up onto the porch and dipped the shirt into the water.

Martin grabbed his sister's arm. "I asked you where this came from."

"I got it at Haney's," Dolly said meekly as she scrubbed at the fabric.

"Spending more of my money?" he yelled. "Without asking my permission?"

"Stop it, Martin." she tried to yank her arm from his grasp. "I bought it with my egg money, not your's."

Her brother snorted. "All the money in this house is my money, stupid twit. You're a female and the government is smart enough to know women can't handle money of their own." He scowled down at Dolly. "Where you been hiding this money and how much do you have?" he asked with a raised brow.

Dolly knew where this was headed. If she told him where she kept her savings, she'd never have anything. Martin would take it to drink and gamble with at the saloon. "I spent all I had on this and sundries for the house," she told him as she fed the shirt through the wringer.

"What did you need that thing for?"

"I was tired of doing the laundry on my knees," she admitted, "and these wringers save my hands."

Martin snorted. "Same lazy, worthless cunny you've always been, Dolly." He watched her shake out the shirt before dropping it into the rinse water. "All I can say is you better get my good shirt clean after letting it get filthy in the yard due to your goddamned clumsiness." He slapped the back of Dolly's head before going back inside. "Then get in here and make my damned breakfast."

"I'll be in in a minute, Martin. I just need to finish hanging the rest of the laundry."

Dolly finished her chores, made breakfast, and was cleaning up the kitchen when someone knocked on the door. She let Martin answer it as he was already in the parlor with the newspaper.

"Bring coffee for me and my friend, Dolly," Martin called.

Dolly peeked into the parlor to see her brother offering a seat on the settee to a well-dressed man of about forty. "I'll have it in a minute, Martin," she called back.

Dolly didn't know the man, but he didn't look like a farmer or rancher, so she poured coffee from the everyday enameled pot into her mama's pretty porcelain coffee service. She proudly arranged the pot on a tray with cups, saucers, creamer, and sugar bowl to carry in and place on the table in front of the stranger. She turned to scurry back into the kitchen when the man spoke.

"Don't go just yet, Miss Stroud," he said in an authoritative tone. "Let me have a good look at you."

Dolly stopped with a questioning glance at her silent brother who simply shrugged. Dolly noticed the sweat on his brow with some concern. She'd heard gruff voices between the men while she prepared the coffee but hadn't heard the exact conversation. She wondered what Martin had gotten himself into this time. Did he owe this man money from a gambling debt? What could the man possibly want with her?

"Very nice, indeed," the man said, appraising Dolly with his eyes. I think she'll do just fine, Mr. Stroud."

Dolly turned to her brother. "Who is this man, Martin and what is he talking about?"

The man stood. "I'm Hiram Davis, Miss Stroud and you are now in my possession."

Dolly's mouth fell open. "Your possession?" She turned to her wide-eyed brother. "What's he talking about, Martin?"

Martin opened his mouth, but no words came out before Davis continued. "I've purchased all your brother's debt," the man said, "including his mortgage on this fine little house at the local bank."

"You mortgaged the house?" Dolly gasped, turning to her blank-faced brother.

"Your brother now has in his hand the note for the five hundred dollars in debt I now hold," Davis said with a grin as he returned to his seat and filled his cup. "You, my dear, are my price for the repayment of that note."

Martin lifted the piece of paper. "You mean you want my sister's hand in marriage for this?"

Davis snorted a chuckle as he reached out to take Dolly's wrist and pull her closer. "I already have a wife in San Francisco." Dolly flinched when the man grabbed her backside. "No, Miss Stroud will accompany me to San Francisco and be put to work at Bainbridge House."

"You want her to work in a hotel?" Martin said with his face contorted in confusion.

"Bainbridge House is not a hotel," Davis said. "It's a very exclusive place where men of unusual tastes come to enjoy the company of beautiful women." He smiled up at Dolly's horrified face. "I assume you're still a virgin?"

"Of course, she's still a virgin," Martin snapped. "I haven't let any of these local hayseeds get at her all these years."

"Even better," Davis said as he continued to fondle Dolly's behind. "I have a very elite group of men who will pay well to deflower a virgin."

"You can't seriously think of letting this happen, Martin," Dolly gasped at her brother who clutched the paper in his hand.

Another man stepped out of the shadows. "He can, and he will," Sheriff Lucas said with a grin as he stared at Dolly. "Mr. Davis has sworn out a warrant of nonpayment against your brother. If he doesn't agree to allow you to leave with him, I will take him into custody, put him in jail, and confiscate this property to be put up for auction to repay the money Mr. Davis has put forth."

Martin's face went pale. "You'd throw me out of my house, Lucas?"

The sheriff grinned. "You and your sister." He walked over and touched Dolly's cheek. "You'd have to put her to work in one of the rooms above the saloon to pay your debts then, Martin, so you're better off lettin' him have her for his damned brothel in San Francisco."

"Martin?" Dolly pled as she tried to get away from Davis and the sheriff.

The sheriff took a pair of shackles from his belt and dangled them in front of her brother. "It's up to you, Martin. Send her off with Mr. Davis to whore in San Francisco or spend the next ten years doing hard labor in the territorial prison."

Dolly watched the change in her brother's face and knew she was lost. Martin would sacrifice her to a life as a whore in order to avoid years of hard labor. "I'm sorry, Dolly," he said in a whimper, "but I can't lose this house and go to prison."

"I'm glad that's settled," Davis said with a broad smile. "Now let's go upstairs to your room and make ready for our trip, Miss Stroud." He smiled at the grinning sheriff as he pulled Dolly toward the stairs. "Stand watch outside, Lucas," the man commanded, "and keep the crowd in tow while Miss Stroud and I get them fired up for the girl's in the wagon."

Dolly followed the man, stumbling on the stairs. She still couldn't believe this was happening to her or that Martin was allowing it to happen.

"This is your room?" Davis asked at the top of the stairs.

Dolly nodded, and he opened the door to the little attic space that had been her room all her life. "Take off your clothes," Davis instructed. He slapped her face when she didn't do as he'd said. "I won't tolerate disobedience."

"I can't undress in front of a strange man," Dolly protested.

Davis replied with a grin as he pulled aside the curtains to her window and slid it open. "Oh, you will, Miss Stroud, and so much more." Dolly heard the voices of men in the alley below her window and wondered what was going on.

❦

Trace sat on his porch stitching together a new holster for a customer when he heard the wagon. He glanced up to see a boxed wagon with barred windows stop in front of Martin Stroud's house. Had someone finally gotten fed up with him cheating at cards and gone to the sheriff and pressed charges? It's certainly about time.

As a boisterous crowd began to gather, Trace stood and dropped his project into the chair. He stepped down off the porch and moved toward the Stroud house to see what was going on. Men laughed and cheered as they stared and pointed up at the window — Dolly's window. Trace's mouth fell open in shock when he got closer and saw Dolly, standing with her naked bosoms pressed against the glass with a pair of man's hands stroking her equally naked body, teasing the crowd when they twined in the red triangle of hair between her thighs.

What in hell's name was going on and how could Martin allow it? Trace pushed through the crowd of men to rush toward the porch where the sheriff stood.

"Damn," Trace heard someone gasped, "If I'd known Dolly sucked cock like that, I'd have pressed Martin a little harder to pay court to her."

Trace shifted his eyes back to the window. The man had Dolly on her knees with his erect cock between her lips. He looked away in disgust.

"There ya are, gents," a man wearing a plaid jacket and a brown bowler hat called out in an Irish accent as he stood pointing at Dolly's window. "Mr. Davis is breakin' in his newest addition." He laughed along with the jeering men.

"Will we get a chance at the redhead when he's done with her?" someone called from the crowd.

"Not today, I fear," the Irishman called back in reply, "but I have a wagon full of willin' lasses here, eager to satisfy all your needs when Mr. Davis is finished with that girlie up there." He laughed and slapped the wagon.

Trace went to the porch and reached for the doorknob. "Hold it right there, Trace," sheriff Lucas commanded and blocked the way. "Just what do you think you're doing?"

"I'm going to stop this travesty," Trace told the sheriff, "just like you or any decent man should have done."

"Why?" the sheriff asked with a grin. "She's a damned filthy whore puttin' on a show for Davis's cat wagon." The sheriff shrugged. "He ain't breakin' any laws I know of."

Trace's mouth fell open. "Dolly's no whore, Lucas. He's gotta be forcin' her to do this."

The sheriff snorted. "I've been here since it started," he said, "and I sure didn't see Dolly puttin' up no fight about it." He stepped off the porch to watch the man stroking his cock between Dolly's lips. "Sure wish I'd known she could take a cock in her mouth like that." He let out a long sigh. "She did squeal some when he shoved it up her tight little ass, though."

The sheriff grinned at Trace. "Go on home and take care of that bulge in your britches or wait and follow the Irishman and his whores. I'm sure one of 'em would be happy to take care of it for ya."

Trace had heard enough. He strode off the porch toward home. He tried to shut the lude comments of the men out of his head as he returned home, but he couldn't. He glanced up at the open window to see Dolly standing again with the man's white fluid running down her quivering chin and the man's hands on her bosoms, playing with her nipples to the enjoyment of the men below.

Maybe he'd been wrong about Dolly. Maybe she was one of those women he'd read about who enjoyed being the center of attention—any sort of attention—and would flaunt their bodies in bawdyhouse shows. Trace tore his eyes away and trudged home.

A few minutes later with Dolly's show ended, the Irishman rolled his wagon past Trace's house, leading the men from town the way St. Patrick was said to have led the snakes out of Ireland and into the sea. Trace glanced back to the Stroud house. Dolly's window was closed, and the curtains drawn. He couldn't believe what he'd seen or that Martin had allowed it to happen. What sort of man allows his sister to be put on display in such a fashion in his own house? He went inside for a drink of water.

When he came back out to finish his project, he saw Dolly follow Davis from the house and climb into his buggy. She wore a dress and bonnet Trace had seen her wear at church several times. It caused his stomach to twist. How could she wear it now after actin like an ungodly whore in front of half the men in town?

When he saw Dolly's tear-stained face in the man's buggy, Trace knew he'd been wrong to think badly of Dolly. She wasn't a whore

15

and he knew she hadn't enjoyed what had been done to her in that window.

The sheriff followed close behind the buggy and doffed his hat at Trace with a broad grin on his face. Trace couldn't believe he'd voted for the bastard.

The big man stood, reached into the house and grabbed the rifle he kept beside the door. He knew what he had to do now. He knew he had to save Dolly from whatever that man had in store for her.

3

Dolly sat in stunned silence. She couldn't believe Martin would let this happen to her. What had she ever done to deserve this?

Tears ran down her red cheeks as Davis pulled the curtains closed. She reached for her dressing gown to cover herself.

"Put on your nicest dress, Miss Stroud," Davis told her. "We leave for Holbrook to catch a train as soon as you're dressed." When Dolly opened her wardrobe and reached for her traveling bag, Davis stopped her. "You won't need any of this other rubbish. We'll put you in proper attire when we reach Bainbridge House." He scratched at his seed drying on her chin. "Clean yourself up a bit, though. You're going to have to learn to swallow or I'm going to need to punish you more severely."

Tears welled in her eyes, remembering the man's hard smacks on her bare behind and his telling her the sound of his hand hitting her flesh aroused him more than seeing her naked body or the anticipation of what was to come. Dolly poured water from the white enameled pitcher into the matching basin, grabbed the washcloth, and scrubbed her face until it turned red. Maybe if she lingered in her room, Davis would tire of waiting for her and leave.

"Don't dally, Miss Stroud," Davis said from outside her door. "I don't have time to waste."

Tears of defeat rolled down Dolly's face and she took a camisole, petticoat, and her best dress from the wardrobe. She'd made the dress for Easter the year before from a pale green cotton fabric printed with white and pink apple blossoms and darker green foliage. She'd trimmed it at the neck and cuffs with white lace and sewn pearl buttons up the front. She'd been proud of the dress and had received many complements on her work from the ladies at church.

Dolly pinned up her red curls and put on the straw bonnet trimmed to match the dress with white lace and green satin ribbons. She left her room and made her way down the narrow attic stairs to the parlor where Davis waited with Martin and the sheriff. She gave her brother a pleading look, but all he did was turn away.

How could he allow this to happen? Did he hate her that much?

"Now don't you look fetching?" the sheriff said with a grin. "I think me and you are gonna have us some fun tonight when we camp."

Davis walked from the settee and stared at Dolly, appraising her. "I suppose that will have to do for the train," he finally said. "Do you want to kiss your brother good-bye? With the lips that were just wrapped around my cock?" he added with a malicious grin at Martin.

"Looked like she does it quite well, Martin," the sheriff goaded her brother. "Have you been training her all these years?"

Martin's eyes went wide, and he gaped at the sheriff's words. "Don't be ridiculous, she's my damned sister, for Christ's sake."

"Very well," Davis said with a chuckle, "let's be off."

"I'm sorry, Dolly," she heard her brother mumble as she walked out the door and more tears welled in her eyes.

She climbed into the buggy beside Davis and he urged the horses into the street. As she settled herself into the leather seat, she saw Trace sitting on his porch with work on his lap. Had he been one of the men who'd stood below her window watching Davis defile her? The thought of it was too much and she allowed the tears to wash down her face.

Davis saw her tears. "There's no sense crying over spilled milk, Miss Stroud," he chided. "This is what your life is now. You're just a whore like any other. Get used to it."

How could she get used to it? How did any woman get used to it? Dolly hung her head as they rolled westward through town. She didn't want anyone to recognize her. She knew she'd never be able to return to Concho after this. Tears of despair rolled down Dolly's face.

"Clean your face, we're almost at the wagon." Davis handed her a clean handkerchief from his pocket. "I need to leave some instructions with that mouthy Irishman and his flunky before we're on our way." He coughed at the dust kicked up along the trail. "He's an ass, but good with the whores and I trust him with my money."

Dolly blew her nose but refused to make conversation with the man. She kept her eyes fixed on the high desert scenery passing by. Davis slowed the buggy and pulled off the trail beside the wagon the Irishman had parked below her window.

Dolly's mouth dropped open at the goings-on around her. Strewn across the clumps of desert grasses and beneath the shade of sprawling cedars were pallets with naked women performing an array of lude acts with the men from town. One woman, years older than most, had been shackled to the large wheel of the wagon and several men stood around her stroking their manhood to release on her naked body, aiming for her mouth. White liquid ran down her cheeks and sagging bosoms.

Dolly wanted to vomit. She held it back as someone recognized her and came running toward the buggy. It was Karl the delivery boy from Haney's Mercantile. "I've got another dollar," the skinny young man offered with the coin in his hand, "if I can give Miss Dolly a poke." He ran up and brazenly rested a hand on Dolly's bosom, squeezing it through her dress and camisole. "You coulda offered me a poke the other day instead of givin' me that nickel," he said and pinched hard when he found her nipple.

"I'm afraid Miss Dolly's cunny is off limits for the time being," Davis said. "And we need to get to Holbrook to catch a train."

Karl reached up to run a dirty finger over Dolly's lips. "That's all right. I'll take her mouth."

The Irishman pulled the young man away from the buggy. "Go stick your cock in Greta's mouth," he said, nodding to the woman chained to the wagon. "Go on, she's free today."

"What's going on there?" Davis asked as he watched Karl slink off to join the men with the woman.

"I think it's time we took ol' Greta up to Crane's," the Irishman said. "She just tried to bite the head of a fella's cock off."

"Oh, my," Davis said with a sigh, "I suppose you're probably right." He sat for a minute watching the men and women around him. "Make the regular circuit around the northern Arizona Territory and then head on up to Colorado and drop Greta off at Crane's." Davis grabbed the Irishman's sleeve. "Don't take less than ten dollars for her, you hear?"

"Yes, sir," he said with his eyes never leaving Dolly. "What about that one? I'll need a replacement for ol' Greta." He licked his lips. "That red hair would certainly be a draw for the wagon."

Davis smiled at Dolly. "I have big plans for Miss Stroud at Bainbridge House, but once she's used up there and no longer in demand, she'll come to you like all the rest."

The Irishman grinned at Dolly. "Me and Pauly will be lookin' forward to it."

"How's the take been?" Davis asked.

"Fair to middlin'." The Irishman took a leather pouch from his jacket and handed it to Davis, who tipped it over and caught the silver coins that poured out.

"Not bad." Dolly watched Davis drop the coins into his pocket. "I'm gonna need this to pay the train fare home for Miss Stroud and I."

The Irishman stuffed the empty pouch back into his trousers when Davis handed it to him, then walked around the skittish horse to stand beside Dolly. "Might I beg a little taste of this gem before you take her west, sir?" he asked and squeezed Dolly's breast the way Karl had. "My willy could sure use a release into some fresh meat. These old cows are gettin' borin'."

Davis rolled his eyes and raised his palm in a dismissive gesture. "Be my guest, but not in her cunny."

The Irishman grinned. "Thanks be to ya, sir," he said and yanked Dolly from the buggy.

⁂

Trace clutched at the stock of his rifle as he watched Dolly be pulled from the buggy and forced to her knees by the vile Irishman and forced to take his cock into her mouth. His blood boiled when the sheriff pulled up her skirts and assaulted her from behind with the men from town watching and pawing at her body.

Why isn't she fighting this? Trace's gut roiled at the sight, but he didn't know who he was more upset with—the men assaulting Dolly or the girl herself. Did she want to be a whore? Had she agreed to all of this? What he knew of Dolly simply didn't fit with what he was witnessing today, and he didn't understand it.

Trace knelt behind some cedars. He was close enough to hear laughter and the men's drunken jeering. He certainly could have heard Dolly cry out in protest, but she hadn't. As he watched the sheriff clutch Dolly's firm, round ass cheeks, Trace's manhood began to thicken and throb in his trousers. He squeezed his eyes shut in shame.

When the sheriff and the Irishman had finished with Dolly, Davis turned away more eager admirers and helped the young woman back into the buggy. With a satisfied grin on his tanned face, sheriff Lucas mounted his horse and they rode on down the trail that would eventually take them to the town of Holbrook.

Trace mounted his mare, shoved the rifle in its leather sheath, and followed after the trio concealed in the thick growth of cedars along the trail. He intended to follow them and at his first opportunity, steal Dolly away from Davis and the sheriff. He shuddered as he contemplated the fact that he might have to kill one or both of the vile men in order to free her, but he didn't care. Trace had sworn to himself and the Lord that he'd never take another life after the atrocities he'd seen during the War. Was saving Dolly worth breaking his vow and possibly damning his soul? He thought about what the life as a whore meant for poor Dolly's soul and decided it was.

4

Dolly found it hard to stop the tears after the encounter at the wagon with the Irishman and the sheriff.

"Will you please stop that infernal blubbering, Miss Stroud?" Davis insisted.

Dolly took the handkerchief he'd given her before, wiped her face, and blew her nose. What did he expect from her after what she'd endured that day? Was she supposed to be happy and smiling? She glanced down and saw the dirty smudges on the skirt of her dress where her knees had dug into the desert's sandy soil and tears stung her eyes again. She'd spent a week making this dress. She knew the dirt would wash out, but the dress she'd worn so proudly before was ruined for her now. She didn't think she'd ever be able to wear it again without her stomach turning.

"Shall I tell you about Bainbridge House and what you'll enjoy there, Miss Stroud?" Davis asked in a cheerful tone.

"If you must," Dolly mumbled.

He turned his head to glare at Dolly. "There is no need to take that impertinent tone with me," he snapped, "and it certainly won't be tolerated at Bainbridge." He smiled when Dolly didn't reply. "You see, my clientele at Bainbridge House require submissive women and most rather enjoy beating them into submission, if need be." He studied Dolly's blank face and smiled again. "There are those, of course, who enjoy more than beating a woman until she submits to his desires." He began to chuckle softly. "As a matter of fact, there are many who enjoy the beating more than the sex act itself. Perhaps your surly attitude will be appreciated after all, Miss Stroud."

"You have a lot of whores in this brothel?"

"Fifteen to twenty at any given time," Davis told her.

"And they're there because they want to be or were they taken as slave labor like me?" Dolly said, glaring at the man in his fancy suit. "How much do these women get paid for their services?"

Davis raised a brow. "If you're worried about the money you'll earn then perhaps you're more of a whore than I thought." He grinned. "I get paid for the services my women provide and the women receive tips if the man appreciates his encounter."

"So you don't pay them at all?" Dolly spat.

"I house them in lovely rooms, dress them in the finest clothes, and feed them better than most of them ever were fed," Davis said. "I assure you, Miss Stroud, the women at Bainbridge house make no complaints."

"They'd probably get their mouths slapped if they did."

"Indeed, they would." Davis grinned. "Indeed, they would."

Dolly, feeling emboldened asked. "Why did you choose me for your brothel, Mr. Davis? Surely there are plenty of women who would have been willing to join your whores in San Francisco. Why did you have to have me?"

Davis turned to stare at Dolly. "You are a lovely young woman, Miss Stroud. Has no one ever told you that?" He flicked the reins to urge the horse into a trot over the dusty trail. "I have clients who require certain attributes in a young woman. I saw you with your brother in the mercantile," he said, "and I was impressed with your submissive attitude toward him. When he told you to fetch something, you fetched it without question or delay." Davis smiled. "And when I questioned some of the others I encountered in town, they insured me you were a church-going young woman of unquestionable," he paused, "purity."

Dolly rolled her eyes as understanding dawned on her. So that's what he was looking for—a virgin. "You wanted a virgin? Why? Don't men want experience in their whores?"

Davis turned his head with a broad smile on his face. "Oh, I intend to see that you have plenty of experience before we reach Bainbridge House, Miss Stroud. Have I not been providing you with experience already?"

Dolly adjusted her aching behind and touched her bruised lips. "I suppose you have."

"Men come to Bainbridge House for entertainment to arouse them for the sex act," Davis explained. "I have a lavish theatre room there with comfortable seating. Men come from all over the continent to be entertained. Some even pay to be part of the entertainment."

"I don't understand," Dolly said with her face twisted in confusion.

"No, I don't suppose you would."

"Before we reach Bainbridge House," Davis said, "I will send out telegrams to several of my very special clients, announcing my find of a fiery redheaded virgin. I will then begin fielding bids."

"Bids? Bids for what?"

Davis chuckled. "Come now, Miss Stroud, you are not a stupid young woman. The bids will be for the opportunity to deflower you on stage in front of the assembled audience."

"What?" Dolly gasped in horror. "That's disgusting."

"It can be," Davis admitted with a grin, "depending upon who presents the highest bid. If it's Mr. Gutierrez from El Salvador, it could be quite brutal. He enjoys a little fight in his woman and likes to draw blood from more than the cunny."

"And men pay to watch such a thing?"

"That and so much more," he said with a sigh. "I offer weekly stage performances with men and women performing sexual acts with one another. Some men enjoy and pay to watch a woman be disciplined while others pay to do the disciplining."

Dolly's eyes went wide. "And the women go along with this?"

"The best reaction from the audience comes when the woman doesn't know what's in store. They enjoy the weeping and begging as she's being beaten and ultimately abused."

"That's disgusting." Dolly couldn't believe what the man was telling her. Surely there couldn't be men in the world like those he described. What sort of monster pays to watch a woman be beaten for his sexual gratification?

"You will come to find, as I have, that men's tastes for the unusual cover the board like so many chess pieces. Some want a simple poke in the cunny and are satisfied, while others can only achieve fulfillment with what some would call horrific acts. I leave that to my friend Crane, however."

Dolly arched a brow. "The man you were sending that Gert to?"

"Sadly, yes," Davis said with a sigh, "Mr. Crane's establishment outside Denver is the last stop for many a whore."

What more could there possibly be?

"While some men enjoy watching a woman being taken or beaten upon the stage," Davis said, "there are others who wish to take it to the next step and see the woman take her last breath. Some will pay a tidy sum to be the one doing the taking, but I won't go that far at Bainbridge House."

Dolly curled her lip. "How very civil of you."

"There's no need to be snide, Miss Stroud." Davis shrugged his narrow shoulders. "Crane and I realized these unique urges in men and have simply found ways to satisfy them."

"At a profit." Dolly shook her head, shuddered, and squeezed her eyes shut at the thought of such horrid things. Was Davis telling her the truth or simply trying to frighten her?

"And a very good profit."

"What does a man have to pay to take my virginity in front of an audience, Mr. Davis?"

"I'll start the bidding at a hundred dollars," he said with a grin, "but I'd expect it to go as high as a thousand for one as lovely as you. Men find redheads irresistible, especially pretty ones."

Dolly's mouth fell open. "And just how much will I get of that thousand dollars?"

Davis grinned. "You'll get a nice room in Bainbridge House, nice clothes to wear, and good food from the kitchen."

Dolly narrowed her eyes. "In other words, not a damned thing."

"Your living conditions will be much improved over this dry, shriveled desert as well as the food." Davis reached for Dolly's hand. "I'm sure you'll be quite happy at Bainbridge House."

Did he honestly think she'd be happy as a whore? Dolly looked out at the green cedars and swaying grasses and sighed. She'd miss the high desert and the open spaces. She didn't know how she'd handle being stuck in a bedroom all day, but she supposed she'd have to get used to it. She couldn't let these men take the house and send Martin to jail.

Dolly still couldn't believe Martin had mortgaged the house. Why? To gamble with and buy fancy silk shirts? He certainly never used any of it around the house. The cook stove smoked and the upholstery on their old settee was practically worn through to the padding.

Dolly had bought the new jute rope with her own money to restring her bed and stuffed the thin pad with chicken feathers from the hens she plucked. Martin had balked at buying new feathers or straw padding at the mercantile. Martin had balked any time Dolly had mentioned needing something new for the house.

He'd called her lazy when she asked for a new churn or frivolous for wanting the settee recovered. Frustrated, Dolly had simply stopped asking for things. If she wanted something, like the new washtubs, she got them with the money she saved and hid from her brother.

Dolly grinned with satisfaction at a memory. When she'd stuffed the mattress pad on her bed and her pillows, she hadn't bothered with Martin's. If he wanted it done, he could pluck the hens himself and reseam the pad and pillows.

A shadow fell across her lap and Dolly glanced up to see the sheriff staring down at her from his saddle. "I think I'm gonna ride out and find a jackrabbit for you to cook up for our supper, Dolly."

He grinned and then bent to speak to Davis. "I got me some plans for this one tonight, Mr. Davis. Sharin' her with that Irish fella has given me some ideas. How 'bout you and me teach the little bitch how to swallow our seed like a proper whore."

"Sounds good to me, sheriff, but remember her cunny is off limits."

The sheriff straightened up and laughed. "I want to choke her with my cock and pump her mouth full of my hot seed." He continued to cackle. "And I want to see her bosoms. How 'bout we strip her naked and have her cook our supper that way?"

"It would certainly save wear on the dress," Davis said, "such as it is."

There was absolutely nothing wrong with her dress, save a bit of sandy soil ground into the knees. What did he mean by 'such as it is'? Dolly was about to say something when the crack of a rifle made her jerk in the seat. Something wet splattered on the side of her face and the sheriff's hat flew off toward the front of the buggy, followed by a good portion of his scalp and brain. Dolly screamed at the horror and brushed at her face to get it off.

"Hang on, Miss Stroud," Davis shouted as the horse, spooked by the gunfire, began to gallop out of control over the rutted trail.

Dolly turned her head to see the sheriff's gray mare trotting along beside them with the bloody corpse of the man slumped in the saddle. Her head went swimmy at the horrific sight and her stomach threatened to empty itself.

Dolly saw Davis struggling with the reins, trying to slow the frantic animal. It had left the trail and the buggy now bounced across the clumps of desert grass as the steed darted around cedars. The buggy hit something and tipped up on one wheel. Dolly screamed and held tight to the canopy, but when it tipped to one side and threw her from it, everything went black.

5

When Trace found the overturned buggy, Dolly wasn't in it. Davis had been thrown across the seat, still tangled in the reins of the lathered animal that stood still hitched and panting with its eyes wide with fear. Davis's head rested at an unnatural angle and Trace knew from his experience in a Confederate medical unit during the war that the man had broken his neck when the out of control buggy had overturned.

But where was Dolly? Trace called her name as he raced back along the tracks the buggy's narrow wheels had made in the sandy soil. He found her in the shade of a cedar. Blood ran down her face from a wound on the right side of her head. Her dress was torn and dirty. It was splattered with blood, but Trace didn't think it belonged to the young woman. The sheriff had been riding close to the buggy and Dolly when Trace had fired his rifle at the crude man, threatening Dolly with more abuse. The splattered blood probably belonged to him.

He checked Dolly for broken bones but didn't find any. He breathed a sigh of relief and began to probe the wound on her head. The scalp was cut and bleeding profusely, but he didn't feel a depression on the skull. He knew that would have been bad.

"I think you just have a bad cut, Dolly," Trace told the unconscious young woman as he tore the ruffled bottom of her petticoat away to use as a bandage.

She was breathing That was the important thing. Trace tore off some of the ruffle and folded it to place over the bleeding laceration. Then he wrapped some of it around her head to keep the pad in place, covering her eyes to keep away gnats and flies. Trace knew from his experience in the field that head injuries could be tricky. She might wake up any minute and be fine or she might not wake up for a week and be a halfwit. Trace stared down at Dolly's pretty face. Or she might never wake up at all.

He went to his horse and got a blanket from the bedroll attached to the saddle he used for hunting trips. When he got it rolled out on a level spot, Trace lifted the unconscious young woman in his muscular arms and laid her down gently.

"I'm so sorry, Dolly," Trace whispered as he held her unmoving hand, "I never gave any thought to spookin' the damned horse and Davis not bein' able to control the animal. I guess I've been livin' around farmers and ranchers too long." He chuckled softly. "I reckon even their wives and daughters could have handled a spooked horse better than that dandy in his fancy suit."

Trace saw buzzards beginning to circle in the blue sky and got to his feet. "I suppose I'd best get to plantin' those two bastards in the ground, Dolly." He spat in the warm sand at his feet. "Not that either of 'em deserve a decent burial for what they did to you. I should just lay 'em out for the buzzards and coyotes to feed on." He knelt again and patted Dolly's hand. After studying her face, Trace bent to kiss her bandaged head. "I'll be back before dark and build us a fire." He got up again and walked toward his horse.

Two hours later Trace returned sweaty and leading the sheriff's horse along with his own mare. He dropped the gun belt he'd removed from the sheriff's body next to Dolly and staked the horses out in a grassy area. He gave them some water from a canteen he'd found on the sheriff's saddle — a saddle Trace had made along with all the tack.

After dealing with the horses and checking on Dolly, who

remained unmoving and unconscious on the blanket, Trace dug a fire pit and started a fire. He didn't want to worry about coyotes or gray wolves coming in to sniff at them in the night.

As the evening began to cool, Trace moved his silent charge nearer to the fire and covered Dolly with the blanket from the sheriff's bedroll, spread horse blankets by the fire, and settled down to rest. Dolly had shown no signs of coming around and that worried him some. Trace wondered if he should try to get the crashed buggy into some sort of order and take Dolly back into town to see a doctor.

The buggy, however, proved to be more than Trace could manage on his own. One of the wheels had been wrenched away from the axle when it went over and would require a skilled wagon man to repair.

Before complete darkness fell, Trace went to Dolly, adjusted her on the pallet and poured some water from the canteen down her throat. He had seen unconscious men die because they hadn't been forced to drink water. A man's body could go without food for an extended period of time, but not water. He supposed a woman was no different. He made a mental note to boil some of the elk jerky he had in his saddle bag to make her a broth in the morning.

"What am I going to do with you now, Dolly?" Trace asked as he stroked her soft, bruised cheek. "I don't think I should take you back to Martin. That bastard, I know, is your brother, but he let this happen to you, and there's no forgivin' that in my way of thinkin'."

His eyes wandered down to watch her chest move up and down as she breathed, lingering on her full bosoms. "You're a mighty beautiful girl, Dolly," he said before averting his eyes from her chest with a bang of guilt. "I suppose I should say a mighty beautiful woman. It's been some time since you were just a girl comin' over to my house to help me out after Lucy died." He bent and kissed her bandaged forehead. "Did I ever thank you for that?" He bushed her forehead with his lips again. "I think you might have saved my life and I thank you for that."

Trace arranged his blankets closer to Dolly, put more wood on the fire and stretched out without removing his boots. He dozed fitfully throughout the long night, rousing several times to check on Dolly's breathing. Coyotes yipped in the distance and once he woke to the howling of wolves.

When he woke the last time, the sun peeked over the eastern horizon. He checked on Dolly again. She was still unconscious, and blood had seeped to the surface of her bandage. Before rising to relieve himself, Trace changed the bandage. After that, he filled a tin pot from his kit with water and dropped a piece of the salty, smoky jerky he made in the smokehouse at his hunting cabin on the mountain into it. Then he boiled some coffee for himself.

He wondered again what he was going to do next. He glanced up at the staked horses. He couldn't very well ride back into Concho with the dead sheriff's horse in tow. He didn't think his conscience would allow him to lie and if he admitted shooting the man, he'd be hung for murder.

Trace strained the coffee through cheese cloth into his dented enameled cup and inhaled the rich brew. He glanced at the sleeping woman and wondered if she liked coffee and how she took it—with sugar, cream, or both.

Trace checked the boiling pot. The water had changed to a soft brown shade and he smiled. That meant the juices from the meat were seeping into the water. He took the pot off the fire and set it aside to cool for Dolly. She needed the nourishment of the hardy broth.

As he poured the broth into his empty cup, Trace stared at the soggy strips of jerky. He gave his head a mental slap and smiled. Why hadn't he thought of it before?

He gently lifted Dolly's head and put the cup to her soft, pink lips. "What do you think about a trip up to my hunting cabin, Dolly? I know you've never seen it but it's real peaceful up there away from everyone."

Trace took his time as he trickled the broth into Dolly's mouth, massaging her throat the way he'd been trained, to make certain she swallowed the fluid without choking. When he'd emptied the cup, he poured the remainder of the liquid into the sheriff's nearly empty canteen to give to Dolly later. He packed up the camp and covered the ashes in the pit with sand. He certainly didn't want to start a brush fire that would blaze through the dry grasses and cedars at an alarming rate and might alert folks to the graves he'd covered the night before.

With the horses packed up, Trace draped Dolly over his horse in front of the saddle, climbed up, and gently lifted Dolly onto his lap with her legs dangling to one side and her head resting on his left chest.

"Well, I guess we're ready to head up the mountain," he whispered into her bright, red hair and urged his mount toward the narrow trail up the mountain, leading to his cabin.

Two hours into their trip, Dolly whimpered and mumbled something into his chest. Hoping Dolly was coming to, Trace stopped his horse and studied her face.

"What did you say, Dolly? Are you wakin' up?" He patted her cheek. "Please wake up, sweetheart," he implored.

"Please don't let them hurt me anymore," the girl mumbled, grabbed onto his shirt, and then settled into Trace's arms again.

"I won't," Trace promised. "I won't let anybody hurt you ever again."

He studied her soft breathing and decided she was now sleeping and not unconscious from the head injury. Trace continued to hold her close as the horse followed the steep trail up the mountain. They'd made the trip together many times and he suspected the animal knew the way without his direction, though he carried Dolly's extra weight and had the other horses on the trail behind.

Trace bent and patted the animal's neck. "Take us home, boy. We need to get this young lady settled."

They had hours of riding ahead of them and would need to spend another night under the stars. Trace hoped the creek still had water in it for the horses because his canteen was almost dry. Dolly would need water again along with the remainder of the broth. His belly growled, and Trace fished into his pack for a strip of jerky. He bit into the smoky meat and tugged off a mouth full. It would have to do him until they reached the cabin where he had a wild hog hanging in the smokehouse.

Dolly didn't know where she was. She wandered aimlessly through a dark landscape. Sometimes she heard a voice she thought she recognized but couldn't place. She trembled with fear and her body ached. How had she come to this place? Was this hell or the Purgatory her Catholic friends talked about? Had God forsaken her for what she'd allowed those men to do to her—for being a whore?

Again, Dolly felt hands upon her body and saw the sheriff's leering grin or Davis's. How had she come to this? Was she sleeping? Was all of this just a bad dream she'd wake up from? Dolly tried to make herself wake up. She wanted so badly to wake up in her room, have a cup of coffee, and see her tidy kitchen. She needed to wake up. She had chores to do. The chickens needed feeding, the garden needed weeding, and she needed to make bread. She had to wake up and get her chores done or Martin would be furious.

She must be awake, but where was she and how did she get to this horrible dark place? It looked as though a dust storm or heavy rain had blotted out the sun. But why was she walking and where was she going?

Pain lanced through her head and her cheek hurt. Dolly saw Davis again and felt his angry slap. What was happening to her? She heard the sheriff's mocking laughter and felt his hands upon her backside as he … she didn't want to think about that stabbing pain again. Dolly heard the soft, comforting voice again, and reached out in the darkness.

"Please don't let them hurt me again," she begged.

The voice said something Dolly couldn't quite understand, but it sounded comforting and familiar—not the voice of Davis or the horrid sheriff. Dolly allowed herself to drift down into the darkness again, but the fear had left her, and she slept.

6

Trace couldn't believe the beauty of her body.

When they reached the cabin, Trace put Dolly on the bed. She hadn't roused again, but her head wound had stopped bleeding. He built a fire in the iron cook stove and warmed some water. He bathed the crusty blood from the wound and changed the dressing again. Dolly's dress was in filthy tatters and splattered with blood. He decided the girl would rest easier out of it.

With trembling hands, Trace unbuttoned the dress and eased Dolly out of it. Her petticoat reeked of urine. It had been three days since the accident, and he'd been forcing water and broth into her.

"I guess it had to go somewhere, huh." Trace said to the sleeping girl with a soft chuckle. "I better get those off you too, and get you cleaned up."

Trace untied the bow at the waist of Dolly's petticoat and pulled the urine-stained garment off over her hips. He tried to avoid staring at the triangle of dark red hair between her thighs, but it proved difficult with her female musk wafting up to his nose. He undid the tiny buttons of her camisole and was amazed at the size of her firm bosoms. He slipped Dolly's bruised arms from the flimsy garment and tossed it to the floor with the petticoat.

With warm water and a soft cloth, Trace washed Dolly's body, lingering on her bosoms. He hadn't put his hands on a naked female body since Lucy had passed two years before. It surprised him that the sleeping young woman's nipples were roused when he brushed over them with the cloth. Against his better nature, Trace touched the hard, pink nubs with his bare fingers. Dolly moaned softly, and he yanked his hand away.

Knowing she'd wet herself, Trace continued down her body with the wet cloth. He rolled her a little and wiped her backside, studying the bruises left there by the sheriff. His fingers had left behind dark evidence of his holding on to her while he assaulted Dolly from behind. Loathing for the man surged though Traces body as he remembered watching from the cedars.

Trace eased her legs apart and used the cloth to clean between Dolly's firm, pale thighs. Her musk aroused him beyond caring and before he knew it, Trace found his finger exploring the moist warm folds of her cunny. His cock throbbed with desire and need as he ran his index finger in and out.

He contemplated simply crawling on top of the unconscious girl and taking what others already had when his finger ran into a barrier inside her cunny. Trace remembered that same barrier in Lucy on their wedding night—her maidenhead. He jerked his finger out of Dolly in shame and stumbled away from the bed. He cursed himself for being no better than the dead men in the desert.

Dolly was still a virgin and he'd wanted to take that from her. He chastised himself for losing control and doing such a horrific thing to the young woman who'd already been forced to endure so much. Trace's cock wilted in his trousers and his face burned with shame. He covered Dolly with the old quilt his mother had made when he was a child and threw out the dirty bath water.

Seeing the dirty clothes on the floor, Trace picked them up and dropped them into a wash tub. He took the water from the pot on the stove and poured it over them, added some shavings from the bar of soap, and left them to soak. He probably wouldn't be able to get all of the blood out of the dress, but he'd do the best he could. Dolly would need something to wear and he had no women's clothes here. He'd done away with the few things of Lucy's some time ago.

Later that afternoon, after a long nap in his chair on the porch, Trace tended to the clothes and hung them on the line to dry. For his supper, he sliced off some ham from the hind quarter of the hog in the smoke house and fried up some of the spongy potatoes from the root cellar. They all had eyes sprouting from them. Maybe tomorrow he'd spade up the garden spot he and Lucy had used and plant them. He missed her so much.

He and Lucy Poe had married in Texas the year before the War began. They were living with her parents when Trace enlisted with the Confederacy. After the fighting ended, Trace returned to Texas to find Lucy alone and grieving. Her parents had both been killed in a Comanche raid of their small farm while Lucy was spending a few days with a friend in Austin.

Trace had bundled up his wife and set out for Arizona where he'd heard good land could be had for the taking. They ended up in the Basque settlement of Concho. It was small and the people friendly. They accepted the Texans eagerly and when they learned of Trace's leatherworking, he found himself in business. A few years later, the Mormons arrived and bought out the Basques, who moved on to California with their sheep.

He and Lucy purchased the house across from the Stroud home and Trace built his saddle shop. He and Lucy had almost given up on having a child after several years of trying without success. Then, seven years into their marriage Lucy announced that she hadn't had her monthly and thought she was pregnant. The doctor confirmed it and they spent the next several months waiting and preparing the house for a little one. Lucy sewed baby clothes and Trace fixed up the attic room as a nursery.

When Lucy's water broke one afternoon while she was cooking supper, the two of them were so excited to hold the new life in their arms. Unfortunately, after ten hours of grueling labor, Lucy died without expelling the child. The doctor told Trace the child had simply been too large for his small wife to give birth to.

That day had been the end of life for Trace and he prayed to die and be buried next to his sweet Lucy and the babe he'd never see or hold in his arms. Lucy had been buried with the child still in her swollen belly.

If it hadn't been for Dolly's almost daily visits, Trace was certain he'd have taken his life. He glanced at the pretty young woman sleeping in his bed. Could he handle losing her too?

※

Dolly woke to the aroma of coffee and the sound of something sizzling in a skillet. She blinked and opened her eyes, but all she saw was darkness. She lifted her hand to her throbbing head and felt a cloth. She moaned and tried to sit up. Did Davis have her tied up somewhere? She could tell she wore no clothes beneath the quilt covering her body.

"Where am I?" she mumbled more to herself than anyone else who might be about.

"Dolly?" a male voice said. A voice she knew she should recognize. "Are you awake?" She felt a hand on her cheek. How are you feelin'?"

Dolly felt an urgent tingling between her legs. "I need the toilet," she said.

"There's a chamber pot under the bed," the voice said.

She tried to sit up, remembered her nakedness, and fell back onto the pillow. "I need my clothes."

"Oh, yah," the voice said with a soft chuckle. "I forgot about that. They were dirty from … eh," he hesitated uneasily, "from the accident and I washed 'em. They're out on the line, but the dress is torn some, I fear."

Dolly screwed up her face in confusion. He'd washed her clothes? Martin, the only man she'd ever had much experience with, would never have washed her clothes. Laundry was a woman's job. The need to urinate became more pressing.

"Would you step outside then? I don't want to wet the bed."

"Ok, yah, sure," he said, and Dolly heard his boots moving away across the wood floor. "The pot is just under the edge of the bed below you," he said before she heard the door open and close.

Dolly waited until she heard his boots on the porch outside before she threw off the blanket. She wasn't certain who this man was, and she couldn't trust that he'd actually gone outside after opening and closing the door. Dolly swung her stiff legs over the side of the warm bed. Her toes touched the floor and her head began to go swimmy. How long had she been asleep? Her joints were stiff, and her muscles ached when she moved.

She waited for her head to clear before sliding off the bed and squatting. She felt beneath the bed until her hand found the enameled chamber pot. She positioned it beneath her and urinated a strong stream with a great sigh of relief. She swore nothing had ever felt so good.

Dolly returned the lid to the pot and slid it back beneath the bed. Her belly clinched as she returned to the bed and covered herself. The smell of the coffee and food made her mouth water. She had no idea how long it had been since she'd eaten.

She heard the door open. "You all done?"

"Yes," she said, clutching the quilt tightly beneath her chin.

Dolly heard his boots on the floor. "I brought you your clothes," he told her as he dropped the garments across her feet, "but like I said before, the dress will need mending some before you can wear it."

"That's all right. I can put on my camisole and petticoat for the time being." She rubbed at her aching head. "If you don't mind seeing a girl in just her underthings."

He snorted. "My Lu … my wife used to run around the house like that all the time—especially in warm weather. I'd reckon most do." She heard him at the stove. "Are you hungry?"

"Starving," she admitted as her belly grumbled.

"I was gonna fry up some potatoes to go with this ham," he told her. "Sorry I've got no eggs."

Dolly smiled. "That's all right. Ham and potatoes sound wondrous. I can't remember when I last ate." She heard him slicing potatoes and then them sizzling in the skillet. "That coffee smells good too."

"I have a bit of sugar here, but no milk," he said apologetically.

"I drink it black," Dolly said. "But I need to dress before going to the table."

"Oh, sure," he said. "I'll put this skillet up on the warmer and go out on the porch while you dress. Just give me a holler when you're done."

Dolly heard him set the skillet on the metal warming rack above the stove and go outside. She reached for the clothes at her feet, found the underthings and slipped them on. She'd dressed in the dark before, but never thought about how difficult it was to button her camisole without her eyes.

She ran her hands over the bandage again and felt the folded cloth over the tender spot above her right ear. She must have knocked her head on something. She had better not take the bandage off just yet.

When she'd tied her petticoat around her waist, she used her hands to find her way to the door, avoiding the hot stove. Dolly found the latch and lifted it to open the door. She smiled when she felt the warmth of the sun on her face and shoulders. The soft breeze carried the scent of pines and she could hear the branches of the big trees brushing together above her head.

"We're up the mountain?"

"At my hunting cabin," he said as he got up from a chair that scooted across the rough wooden planking of the porch. He took her arm at the elbow. "Let's go back in, Dolly, so I can finish breakfast. I'm starvin' too."

Things were still jumbled together in her head and Dolly still couldn't place the man's voice, though she knew she should. She didn't want to ask for fear of embarrassing him. He must think she knew who he was already. Who did she know that had a hunting cabin on the mountain and why did he bring her here? Had he been one of the men below her window? Had he already used her because he thought she was just a whore? Tears stung her eyes as the man guided her to a chair and helped her to sit. Her hands brushed over a smooth tabletop.

She heard him back at the stove and a few minutes later he set a cup in front of her. "Here's your black coffee, ma'am," he said and put her hand on the cup. "Careful," he warned, "It's hot."

Dolly added her other hand to the metal cup and lifted to her lips with stinging fingers. She blew on the hot liquid a few times after testing it with her tongue. She took a tentative sip and swallowed. The warm liquid running down her throat to her belly was sublime and she quickly took another.

"This is really good," she told him. "I was wishing for coffee in my dream."

"What do you remember?" the man asked. She heard him turning the potatoes in the skillet with something metal. "Do you recall the accident?"

Dolly took another mouth full of coffee as she searched her memory. Accident? What sort of accident? She suddenly remembered the dust, the buggy bouncing through the desert, and the headless sheriff slumped across his horse.

"Davis," she gasped. "You're not Davis. Where is he?"

"In a grave beside that bastard Lucas down in the desert."

Lucas? Oh, Sheriff Lucas. He had helped Davis and Davis had let him assault her. Dolly held back the tears stinging her eyes. Both of them were dead now? Dolly couldn't say that saddened her any. She remembered the gunshot then, and the sheriff's hat tumbling into the trail along with his bloody scalp. She touched the side of her face where his blood had splattered. Then the horse bolting and pulling the buggy into the cedars. Davis told her to hang on as he struggled with the reigns of the bouncing buggy.

"The buggy tipped over," Dolly finally said. "All I remember after that are dark dreams … and …"

"And?" he asked as he set a plate of hot food in front of her.

"And your voice."

"You're safe now, Dolly, so eat up."

Dolly found a fork on the plate and dug into the steaming potatoes. The first bite tasted heavenly. She hardly chewed before swallowing. Her next bite was of salty ham and it tasted equally good. That she chewed, enjoying the smoky juices of the meat. Dolly swallowed another drink of coffee before taking another bite. "This is so good," she mumbled between bites. "Thank you."

"Sorry I don't have any bread to go with it," he said. "I'll go into Vernon tomorrow for some supplies."

Dolly emptied her plate. "Don't be sorry. This is wonderful." She took another sip of coffee and ran a hand over the bandage. "I guess I hit my head when I was thrown from the buggy?"

"You were lucky," he said. "Davis broke this neck."

"Oh, my," Dolly said with a soft sigh, "but I can't really say I'm sorry about it after what that man said he had planned for me." Tears began to soak the cloth over her eyes as Dolly began to sob. Her next words were barely recognizable. "Or what he'd already done."

He pulled Dolly's chair away from the table and swept her up into his strong arms. "Don't you think on that anymore," he told her.

Dolly began to relax. He took her chin in his hand, tilted her head up and kissed her mouth. Dolly had never been kissed like that before. Martin had never allowed any of the boys or men in town to court her. She relaxed her lips and responded to the kiss by allowing his probing tongue into her mouth.

She wanted to know who she was kissing. she reached up and pulled the cloth away from her eyes. The light stung them, but she need to know who this man was. She pulled away from the kiss and gasped. "Trace?"

Her head went swimmy again and Dolly fell into darkness once more.

Trace caught her as she crumpled in his arms. "Was my kissin' really that bad, Dolly?"

7

Dolly woke to an empty cabin. Where was Trace?
Dolly rubbed at her dry eyes before bolting up in the bed and staring around the one room cabin. Had the man who saved her really been Trace Anderson? She slid off the bed and squatted to find the chamber pot again. Gazing around the dim cabin, Dolly wondered where the man was now.

Tears stung her eyes again when she thought about the jeering crowd of men below her window. Had Trace been one of them? She thought back to the condition she'd found herself in when she'd first woken up. Had he taken a turn with her while she lay unconscious? Was Trace that kind of man? Dolly didn't think he was.

Trace had attended the Baptist Church every Sunday. Tears slid down her face. She'd attended the same church every Sunday, but she was no better than a whore now. Why should she expect him not to act like a whoremonger when he had a whore in his bed? Now she knew why he hadn't taken her back home to Concho. He hadn't wanted to be seen bringing her back to her brother's.

Dolly dashed the tears from her cheeks and took a deep, cleansing breath. There was no reason to dwell on it now. She moved her eyes around the small cabin. The walls were built of hewn logs with chinking between them to keep out the cold. She saw three windows. One had been set into the wall the bed stood along and the others on either side of the wide door. Red gingham curtains betrayed Lucy's touch here. The door had been constructed of pine planks with boards in the shape of a Z binding them together. The floor was pine plank and sanded smooth.

On the wall across from the bed stood a tall wardrobe made from cedar boards. It had two doors and below those, two deep drawers. On the same wall as the wardrobe sat a washstand with an enameled metal pitcher and bowl. Linen cloths hung on hooks—one for washing and one for drying. Between one of the windows and the door stood a hall tree with a jacket hanging from one of the hooks. The cook stove which must also be the heat source in the cabin, as there was no fireplace, stood on the same wall as the headboard of the bed. A dry sink and pie safe stood together between the stove and the wall with the door were she saw two chairs with a table between them for a small parlor. The plank table and chairs where they'd eaten their breakfast sat roughly in the very center of the cabin. Dolly noticed that Trace had filled a Mason jar with water and wild flowers and set it in the center of the table. Had he done that for her?

Dolly could tell the place had not seen the attention of a woman since Lucy had died. The curtains hung with dust, the glass in the window was smudged, the top of the stove was greasy, and cobwebs hung from the rafters. She knew how she'd be occupying her days for a while.

Dolly wandered over to the wardrobe and cracked it open. She saw men's shirts and a gray woolen jacket. Brass buttons on the sleeve were stamped with the insignia of the Confederacy. Had she known Trace fought for the South in the War? Feeling guilty about snooping, Dolly closed up the wardrobe and went to the dry sink where Trace had stacked the breakfast dishes.

She poured water from a bucket into a pan and set it on the stove. The least she could do was wash the dishes. After drying and putting the plates and cups away. Dolly found some flour in a bin in the pie safe, tins of baking powders, and a bowl. She used the bacon fat from breakfast and mixed up a batch of biscuits. She had to use water rather than milk, but she thought they'd turn out all right.

As Dolly was taking them from the oven, Trace came in with his rifle flung over his shoulder and a skinned rabbit in his hand.

"Did you make biscuits?" he asked with his eyes wide. "I hope you sifted that flour. It was probably full of weevils." He grinned. "I haven't bought fresh in a while."

"I did," she admitted. "Do you want that rabbit fried? If you do I'm gonna need some lard. I used up all the bacon fat in the biscuits."

"I have a big crock of lard I rendered from that hog down in the cellar. There may be some butter too if it hasn't gone rancid."

Dolly smiled. "Do you have any vegetables hidden out in that cellar?"

Trace handed Dolly the skinned rabbit. "I'll go see what's left. I generally come up here and put out a garden, but since Lucy passed it hasn't been the same. She did cannin' and picklin'." Trace shrugged. "I tend to eat down at The Outpost if I want a hot meal now."

The Outpost was the only restaurant in Concho. Dolly had eaten there with her parents as a child, but since their deaths, Martin had kept her confined to the house, cooking his meals. Not once in the last ten years had he taken her out to eat. She'd attended some church picnics and potlucks, but that had been about it. He, on the other hand ate out at restaurants and saloons all the time, leaving Dolly at home with a full supper cooked and waiting for him.

Trace returned from the cellar with a crock of creamy, white lard, a much smaller one of butter that was not rancid, and a basket filled with spongy carrots and potatoes.

"Can you work with that?" he asked.

Dolly stood at the dry sink, cutting up the rabbit. "Indeed, I can," she said with a smile.

"I'll leave you to it then. I'm going to turn over the garden. Those potatoes need to go into the ground before the season gets too far along.

Dolly set the rabbit pieces aside and peeled the carrots and potatoes. She put them in separate pans with water and set them on the stove to boil. Dolly dusted the rabbit with flour, some crushed garlic she found in the cabinet and salt after she'd scooped lard into the deep skillet and set it on the stove. An hour later, she summoned Trace in for a meal of fried rabbit, mashed potatoes with gravy, carrots, and biscuits.

"Damn, this looks good," he gasped when he saw the table set with everything Dolly had prepared.

Trace filled his plate, buttered two warm biscuits, and dug in. He held up a piece of the rabbit. "How do you get it crispy like this?"

Dolly smiled as Trace bit into the crusty meat. "It's a special trick my mama taught me when I was a girl. You've got to roll it in the flour, dip it in milk … or water, and then roll it again in the flour."

Trace grinned and shook his head as he chewed. "I sure wish your mama had been around to teach Lucy that trick. She could never get her chicken to turn out like this. It usually stuck to the skillet or burned."

"It takes some practice. Eat as many biscuits as you want. I already set some side for breakfast." Dolly scooped some gravy over her potatoes.

"I'd get fat as a Summer tick, eatin' like this every day." Trace smiled. "Your mama would have been proud."

Dolly's face darkened at the thought of her mama and what had happened with Davis. "I seriously doubt that. My mama was a devout Christian woman and wouldn't be proud of what her daughter has become." She squeezed her eyes shut against more tears.

Trace reached over and took Dolly's hand. "Nothing that happened was any of your doin', Dolly." He took a bite of carrot and chewed. "Why did you leave with that Davis character anyway?"

"I had to," she said, "or the sheriff was going to send Martin to prison."

Trace arched his brow. "Why would the sheriff have sent your brother to prison and what did Davis have to do with it?"

"He bought up all of Martin's debt," Dolly explained, "and he threatened to have Martin thrown out of the house and sent to prison for not paying his debts." Dolly swallowed some water. "He said he'd forgive all of Martin's debts if he'd agree to let me go with him to his brothel in San Francisco."

Trace's face had turned bright red. "And your worthless, no good brother agreed to that?"

"He had no choice," Dolly said with a shrug. "It was agree or prison. Martin wouldn't have done very well in prison, Trace. I couldn't let that happen to him after everything he's sacrificed for me since Mama and Daddy died."

Trace snorted. "Martin Stroud hasn't sacrificed a damned thing and he hasn't worked a day of his life." Trace squeezed Dolly's hand again. "I knew your Daddy, Dolly. He was a thrifty man and a dammed hard worker. He put every penny he could in the bank and when he died, he had a pretty good sum there and that house all paid for. It all went to you and Martin after he died, and Martin squandered it all on gambling, booze, and women." Trace stared across the table at Dolly. "Did you know that?"

"Martin mortgaged the house," Dolly mumbled, "and there's no money left in the bank."

Trace shook his head. "He sure didn't spend it on the upkeep of your house. When was the last time it saw fresh paint?"

Dolly thought about the faded and chipping blue paint of the house once thought to be the prettiest in town and frowned. "I've begged him to paint the house and take it back to the one Mama was so proud of, but he always says we don't have the money for a painter."

"And, of course, he's too damned lazy to buy the paint and do it himself," Trace said with a snort.

Dolly furrowed her brow with a grin on her face. "I'd hate to see how that would turn out. We'd probably end up with a white house trimmed in blue and all the window glass painted over." She giggled as she pictured it in her mind.

"It's good to see you smile again, Dolly." Trace took her hand again. "You have a beautiful smile."

Dolly felt her cheeks begin to burn. His hand on hers felt good. No man had ever given her a complement like that before. "Thank you, Trace." Her mind went blank. What should she say to him? Give him a complement on his smile? That sounded silly.

Dolly groped for something to say. "I saw your gray jacket in the wardrobe today. I never knew you fought in the War — for the South."

Trace's face darkened a bit. "I was a Texan," he told her, "and you don't get much farther south than Texas in this country. What were your sympathies?" he asked uneasily.

"We came from Kentucky," Dolly replied, "and the War was the reason we came to Arizona. Daddy's sympathies were with the Union. He thought it was terrible that the country was being torn apart by a few hotheads in Alabama." She took a deep breath before continuing. "He sided with the Republicans in the state and wanted to join the Unionists, but Mama didn't want to see us in a War at all and insisted we go west where there was no fear of the War reaching." She studied Trace's face as he digested her words and emptied his cup. She took both cups to the stove and refilled them. "Are you a sympathizer with slavery?" she finally asked the question that had plagued her since she'd recognized those brass buttons on the jacket. "Daddy would never use another human in that fashion."

Trace grinned. "I imagine Martin had thoughts in the other direction. He's been usin' you as his private servant for as long as I can recall."

Dolly set the fresh cup of coffee down in front of him, shrugged, but didn't say anything more. She could see how he might think that, but she thought she owed it to her brother to take care of the house — and him. Why had she thought that? Was it a fact or was it because Martin had always told her she owed it to him?

Trace interrupted her thought. "Slavery wasn't really the reason for the War," he told her in an authoritative tone, "well, it was, but not how you're thinkin'." He cleared his throat, took a sip of the coffee, and then continued. "It was more about States' Rights," he explained. "The Southern States had all ratified the issue of slavery. The voters had all approved it and it was a recognized law of the land."

"A reprehensible law," Dolly choked.

"But a law none the less. It was the Confederacy's belief that Lincoln and his Congress in Washington DC had the right to strike down and outlaw the practices of an individual state when its people had voted for and approved said practices."

"Well," Dolly quipped "Certainly not all the people, or are you one of those who believe Africans are not people at all, but more like apes than humans?"

"Certainly not," Trace said with his eyes wide. I was simply tryin' to explain that the real dispute wasn't slavery itself, but the rights of the states to decide whether they wanted to allow it within their borders or not." He took another sip of the coffee. "And, no, neither me nor my family ever owned slaves. Daddy had some hired men who'd fled to Texas and had once been slaves, but he paid them like any other hand on the ranch."

Dolly smiled. "That's good to know."

Trace popped the last bite of biscuit into his mouth. "If the political discussions are over for the night," he said with a smile, "I think I'll take my bedroll to the stable and bed down for the night." He stood, bent and kissed Dolly's head. "I plan to ride into Vernon in the mornin' for supplies. Is there anything pressin' you need?"

"Do you have a needle and thread here somewhere? I'd like to try to mend my dress."

"Is that thing even fixable?" he asked with a raised brow. "I think there's a little wicker basket up on the shelf in the wardrobe," he said. "It was Lucy's and it's probably pushed way to the back."

Dolly grinned. "It had better be fixable unless you have six yards of dress fabric hidden around here somewhere, so I can make one." She motioned to her camisole and petticoat. "It's the only thing I have to wear."

Trace smiled at Dolly. "I'm certain the sewing basket is up in the wardrobe. If you think of anything else you need, you can tell me at breakfast." He opened the door and stepped out into the twilight.

Dolly stared at the table full of dirty dishes. She'd cooked him a big meal and he hadn't even asked if her could help her clean up. Was he really all that different from Martin or any other man? She got up and cleared the table. She smiled at the empty bowls and plates. Trace had emptied every one of them.

By the time Dolly had washed and dried all the dishes, it was too dark in the cabin to search for Lucy's sewing basket. That would be a job for tomorrow. She was tired, and her head was throbbing Dolly relieved herself and crawled into the comfortable double bed. She wondered for a minute what it would feel like to have the big man lying beside her. Was it right for him to be sleeping outside in the stable while she took his bed?

She drifted into sleep thinking about his kiss that morning.

8

Trace woke stiff and sore in the loft of the stable, crowded with more horses than it was built for.

He'd fallen asleep almost as soon as he'd laid his head down after a day of working up the garden patch and Dolly's amazing supper. He'd never imagined the girl could have done so much with so little to work with. He smiled and wondered what she could have done with more. Lucy had been a descent cook and had managed to keep his belly full, but Trace didn't think she could have come close to doing what Dolly had last night.

After feeding the horses, Trace went to the cabin and the aroma of bacon met him at the door. He hadn't expected her to be up yet, much less have breakfast started.

"Mornin'," he said as he walked into the cabin where Dolly already had the table set and stood at the stove, forking bacon onto a plate.

"Good morning," Dolly greeted in a cheerful tone. "I hope you slept all right out there."

"Well enough," he told her as he poured water into the basin.

Dolly turned back to the stove when Trace removed his shirt and began to wash.

"We've got no eggs or milk," she said, "but I'm making some flapjacks for breakfast just the same."

Trace grinned. Flapjacks made without eggs or milk were bound to be as flat and tough as one of Mr. Goodyear's buggy tires.

"If you'll get some yeast and fresh flour," Dolly said, "I'll make some fresh bread."

"Yeast bread would be right nice. Lucy always made sourdough."

"I can make a starter for sourdough, if you'd prefer it," Dolly said.

"Yeast is fine," Trace said as he slid a razor over his cheek. "It's actually what I prefer. My mama made her bread with yeast."

"Mama taught me both ways," Dolly told him, "but the sourdough starter is so messy."

Trace rinsed his face and patted it dry. "Did you find Lucy's sewin' basket?"

"I haven't looked yet." Dolly set a plate of flapjacks and crispy bacon on the table. I found the side of bacon in the smokehouse, though," she said with a grin.

"I didn't expect you to make breakfast for me," Trace told her.

Dolly shrugged. "I was hungry and certainly wasn't going to cook just for myself." She filled his cup with coffee and set the pot on the table. "I put some bacon between those biscuits for you to take with you on your trip to Vernon. I don't know how far it is from here or how long it will take you to get there." Dolly smiled. "I thought you might have need of a bite to eat along the way there or back."

"It'll take a good three hours to get there from here," Trace said. "Shoppin's an all-day affair on the mountain, I fear. I probably won't be back until late this afternoon some time." Trace slathered butter on his warm flapjacks, amazed she'd managed to make them light and fluffy. Some women were like wizards in a kitchen. Dolly must be one of those gifted with that magic.

"I couldn't find any syrup," Dolly said as she smeared something red onto her flapjacks, "but I found a crock of raspberry preserves." She pushed the crock across the table to Trace who did the same.

"There might be a tin of syrup down in the root cellar."

"Where's that?" she asked before testing her coffee. "I want to see what I have to work with for supper tonight."

Trace nodded toward the wall with the wardrobe and washstand. "Out that way between the cabin and the stable." He smiled. "You're more than welcome to make an inspection of the entire place. The outhouse is back that way in the woods some." He nodded toward the bed.

"Good. I need to empty my chamber pot." Dolly crinkled her nose in a distasteful manner.

"I can do that before I leave," Trace offered eagerly.

"It's my mess," Dolly told him, "and I'll clean it up. Where do you get fresh water?"

Trace nodded again toward the wall with the wardrobe. "There's water in the rain barrels around the cabin and there's a spring-fed creek out behind the stable a few hundred yards. Follow the path but be mindful of the rocks. There are sometimes snakes sunnin' themselves there."

Dolly furrowed her brow. "I'll keep that in mind and use up the water in the barrels first."

Trace arched a red brow. "What exactly do you have in mind for today? I thought you were going to sew on your dress."

"I am," she said, "but first I'm going to wash the dishes and then tend to this dirty floor. Where do you keep the broom and mop?"

Trace gave her an uneasy grin. "Hidden between the wardrobe and the wall, so I don't have to see them and be reminded I should be usin' one or the other."

Dolly glanced at the dingy floor with dust-bunnies in the corners. "Or both of them."

Trace stuffed the last of his flapjacks into his mouth followed by the last of his coffee, smiled, and stood. "I'd better get goin'. It's a long ride and I fear it's gonna be a hot one today."

Dolly went to the stove where she retrieved a cheesecloth sack and took it to Trace. "Here's your lunch."

"Thank you, Dolly, that's so thoughtful." He took the sack from her hand, grabbed her wrist and pulled her closer. He took her chin, tilted up her head and kissed her mouth again.

He felt her relax and open up to his kiss. Her lips were warm and soft. She tasted like coffee sweetened by the raspberry jam on her flapjacks. She lifted her arms and wrapped her hands around his head, twining her fingers into the hair at the base of his skull.

Trace felt his cock beginning to stiffen and throb with desire for the pretty woman in his arms. He began to run his hand up and down Dolly's back. He longed to touch her silken skin again and found the bottom of her camisole. She flinched when his hand ventured inside to touch her back and he pulled away in shame for his inappropriate boldness.

"I'm sorry," he gasped and stormed out of the cabin.

Well, at least that kiss hadn't flustered her so much, she swooned. His cock had stopped throbbing by the time Trace had saddled his horse and ridden toward Vernon. Had she liked the kiss? Had it stirred her the same way it had stirred him? Trace was certain it had. He'd felt her nipples harden against his chest through the thin fabric of her camisole. He'd wanted nothing more in the world than to lift the woman into his arms and carry her to the bed. He longed to taste more than her mouth. Would she have allowed it the way she'd allowed those others to violate her? The images of Dolly being used like a whore continued to trouble Trace. If she were a whore, she'd allow him between her legs without a fuss and if she fussed, he'd know she wasn't. Trace resolved to test that theory tonight.

Questions about Dolly's response to his kiss plagued him as he passed the farm of Helga Stynegaard, an old Norwegian woman some regarded as a witch because of her odd ways and her herbal medicines. Trace had always liked her husband, Fredrick, though the old man let his wife order him around. Trace bought milk from them when he was on the mountain and would get some for Dolly on his way back to the cabin.

He thought about Dolly's lips all the way into the tiny logging encampment of Vernon, where a two story clapboard building housed the Stanford Mercantile, a business that supplied the local settlers and loggers with goods. They'd also drilled a deep well that had hit good water and the Stanfords filled barrels of it for the families at a minimal price.

Inside the building, Thelma Stanford greeted Trace with a warm smile and a hug. "What can I help you with today, Trace? It's really good to see you again. Up for the summer?"

The question caused Trace some anxiety. Was he up her for the summer or up here for good? Could he ever return to Concho and worry about being accused of murdering Sheriff Lucas?

Dolly could never return to that town where he was sure she'd already been branded a whore. Could he risk leaving her on the mountain all alone?

She'd never be able to endure the harsh winter on the mountain where snows could be counted in feet some years rather than inches and the temperatures could drop well below zero.

Trace smiled. "The summer for certain. I'll be needing a fairly large order today."

"Did you bring leatherwork to trade this year?" Thelma asked with a smile. "We can always use bridles and harness straps."

Trace generally brought a supply of leather goods along to use as trade goods for the summer. "Not this year, I fear. The trip up was a rather hurried affair this year."

"Cash or on account then?" the woman asked with her smile fading.

Trace felt the weight of the sack of leather coins he'd found on Davis's body before burying it. "Silver, ma'am. I don't hold much with putting things on account."

Thelma's face brightened again. "Do you have your list written out or have you put it to memory?"

❧

Dolly started her day, after Trace's kiss, with the dishes. After washing and drying them, she tended to the floor. The cabin featured two large braided rugs — one on the parlor area floor and one in the kitchen. Another smaller oval rug ran along the bed. All were heavy with sandy dirt. She dragged them out to the porch and draped them over the banisters to beat later.

Dolly found the broom and mop where Trace had told her they'd be. She swept the pine boards as best she could, used the broom to knock down the cobwebs from the rafters, and swept again. She mopped the floor using the water left in the wash pan from her dishes and threw the nasty brown water out when she'd finished and refilled the pan with clean water to rinse the floor.

Dolly opened all the windows to let in a breeze while she swept the porch and beat the poor rugs. Upon closer study, she could tell they'd been made of colorful cloth, but were now dingy and brown. She thought she'd hang them over the clothesline the next time it rained to see if it would wash away some of the dirt.

It felt good to be busy, but her mind buzzed with that kiss. She tried to shut her mind to it, but it gnawed at her brain like a mouse on a lump of cheese. This kiss had inflamed her like nothing she could have imagined. She'd read about that sort of thing in the romance novels she bought at the apothecary but had never thought to experience it. Her nipples had throbbed as well as that tiny spot above her cunny. What did it mean? In her novels it always meant the heroine was in love and ready to give herself to the man. After what she'd gone through with Davis, Dolly didn't know if she'd ever be able to tolerate the touch of a man on her skin again. Just look how she'd flinched away from Trace's hand on her back. It had scared him away and Dolly doubted he'd ever want to touch or kiss her again.

The Irishman stormed out of Crane's place with a frown on his face. He'd delivered Greta to the man who'd only wanted to give him five dollars for the old, used-up whore. Davis had demanded ten, but they'd settled on eight and a bottle of prime Irish whiskey. Davis didn't need to know about the whiskey or that he hadn't received the whole ten dollars. He'd really wanted to hang around and watch what Greta had coming, but Crane told him the event wouldn't take place for two weeks at least.

The sluts in the wagon were quiet for a change. None of them wanted to be the next one turned over to Crane. "Any word from Davis?" Pauly asked, as he stepped out of the wagon where he'd probably just had his cock sucked again. The man's cock was never satisfied.

The Irishman shook his head. "I telegraphed him in San Francisco from Denver and told him to reply here, but Crane hadn't heard anything."

"You think something happened to him in Arizona to make him miss his train?" Pauly grinned. "Maybe he changed his mind about the redhead and is holed up with her somewhere suckin' on them big bosoms and strokin' his cock in her pretty little cunny."

The Irishman grinned. He'd fantasized about doing just that himself, but he knew Davis. The little slut's unmolested cunny was worth hundreds to him at Bainbridge House, and the greedy bastard wasn't about to pass that up for a poke he could have for nothin' once she'd been deflowered in the theater by one of his perverted clients and become an earnin' whore in his brothel.

"I got to admit, Pauly, my boy," the Irishman said with a slap on the other man's back, "that I'm eager to plant my Irish cock in that redhead's holes, but alas, it's gonna have to wait till she's used up at Bainbridge House in a year or two."

Pauly frowned. "Maybe we'll run across something else. I saw a sweet little Mex gal I'd liked to have trained up while we were down in Arizona." He glanced at the wagon. "I'm gettin' tired of this lot."

"Maybe we'll look her up," the Irishman said with a grin. "We need to head back that way and see if we can find out what's become of our Mr. Davis and his little redheaded slut." Davis glanced at the wagon. "You hitch up the horses while I drain my weasel into little Bella."

Pauly grinned. "Pick another. I just filled Bella up and you don't want to overfeed any of 'em."

The Irishman laughed as he strode to the wagon. Maybe he'd give all eleven cunny's a stroke or two and choose the one who begged the best to fill her mouth. His cock grew stiff at the thought. He loved to hear the bitches beg and he couldn't wait to have that redhead on her knees in front of him again. Her mouth, with her tears rolling down her cheeks, had been so sweet. It had taken all his control to hold it back until that filthy sheriff had shot his load into the blubbering slut's tight little ass. He was going to enjoy having that one on his wagon once Davis had finished with her.

9

Trace returned late that evening, his horse loaded down with surprises.

Dolly has a supper ready to equal the one the night before. She'd sliced a roast off the hog in the smokehouse and baked it with potatoes, onions and carrots she'd gathered from the root cellar to make a savory, smoky gravy. She'd also baked a pie with the shriveled apples she'd found.

While she put the feast on the table, Trace carried in what he'd hauled home. Dolly was excited to see a sack of flour, another of cornmeal, two cones of brown sugar, a fresh bar of soap, tins of yeast and other baking powders, a crate with two dozen eggs, a bag of fresher potatoes, and some smoked chickens.

"This is amazing," Dolly gasped when she saw it all.

Trace grinned at her broad smile. "Just wait until you see the rest."

Her blue eyes went wide. "There's more?"

"Let's eat first," he said, staring at the table. "I'm starved, and this is what looks amazing."

Trace took his set and began filling his plate. "Where the hell did you find fresh greens?" he asked as he scooped up the tender leaves Dolly had wilted with hot bacon fat and vinegar. He stuffed a fork full into his mouth and chewed. "Oh, my lord," he sighed with satisfaction as he chewed, "wild onions too?"

Dolly's cheeks colored. "I found them down by the creek. Is that a wild plum thicket down there?"

Trace nodded as he ladled the thin, brown gravy over his meat and potatoes. "Yep, Lucy used to make plum butter from them every summer. Did you see any green ones yet?"

"The branches are loaded with them."

"They don't get none too big," he told her, "but they're tasty."

"I look forward to tasting them." Dolly sipped water from her cup. "How was the ride?"

"Long and hot," Trace said, rolling his eyes. "I'd never have made it without those biscuits you fixed up for me."

Dolly's cheeks flushed again. "I'll remember that for the next trip." She filled her mouth with greens. "So, what else did you get?" she asked like a child who' been waiting all day to open a gift.

Trace didn't imagine her worthless brother, Martin, had been much of the giving type. Dolly probably hadn't received a gift since her parents paseed, ten years ago. Was he being cruel to make her wait while he filled his belly?

"I stopped at the Snydergaard farm up the road and ordered some things. Fredrick will bring them on his buckboard in the morning." Trace watched her smile fade a little. "Can you wait that long?"

Dolly took a deep breath and grinned. "I suppose I'll have to, won't I."

They finished their meal over chit-chat. When their plates were empty along with the bowls, Dolly rose. "I have a little surprise for you too," she said with an impish grin and walked toward the stove.

Trace emptied his cup of coffee. *What more could she possibly have to surprise me with after such a fine meal?*

Dolly walked back with a pie in her hands and Trace's mouth fell open. "You made a damned pie?" he gasped. "With what?"

"I found some withered apples in the cellar," she told him as she cut the pie. "They were too soft to eat outright, but fine for a pie, and I found a few tins of baking spices up in the cabinet."

Trace held out his plate for Dolly to put the slice of pie upon. "Those were Lucy's and old as hell," he said, "but I'm glad I never threw them out." He forked a bite of the warm pie into his mouth and closed his eyes, savoring the flavor. "Damn, that's good."

Dolly refilled their cups and sat down to enjoy her pie. "I'm glad you like it and the meal."

"Like it?" he said with his eyes wide. "This is the best meal I've had in years," he hesitated and then added in a sheepish tone, "except for the one yesterday. That was great too."

"It's the least I could do," she said as she touched the bandaged spot on her head, "after you saved me from certain death or worse at the hands of Davis and the sheriff."

It was Trace's turn to blush. He'd been thinking there was something else Dolly could do, but now he felt embarrassed with himself and ashamed. Dolly wasn't that kind of girl. Her sense of indebtedness to her brother forced her into the situation with Davis and Trace refused to blame Dolly anymore.

He finished his pie and coffee before standing. "I need to bed down the horse," he told Dolly as she cleared the table and then walked out into the dark.

❧

Dolly watched him leave. Did he even say thank you for the meal? It's dark now, but did he even notice the clean floor, the beaten rugs, or the curtains I shook out? She set a pan of water on the stove to heat. She was bone tired and her head ached, but she'd never gone to bed with a messy kitchen and she had no intention of doing so tonight. Dolly spent the better part of an hour washing the dishes and scrubbing the kitchen.

In that time, Trace had not returned. Maybe he had been tired and had simply gone to bed. Had he even said he was coming back in? As Dolly turned back her bed, Trace stepped inside. He held something in his arms.

"I found something I forgot." Trace walked through the dark parlor and around the pie safe into the light of the lamp.

Dolly gasped when she realized what was carrying. "You brought me fabric?"

Trace handed her the bolt of green chintz and she ran her hand over the soft cotton fabric.

"You said you needed six yards for a dress," he said with a grin, "but Mrs. Sanders gave me the whole ten yards for the price of six."

Dolly dropped the bolt onto the bed and ran to Trace, wrapping her arms around his neck and kissing his mouth. She pulled back for a minute. "Nobody's ever given me such a fine gift before." Tears welled in her eyes. "Thank you."

Trace ran his hand through her hair. "I thought the green would look nice with your hair."

Dolly kissed him again. She parted her lips and allowed his tongue in. She was soft and warm in is arms and caressed the back of his head, playing with the hair at the base of his skull that sent chills running down his spine. He could feel her rigid nipples pressing into his chest and he wondered if he dare do what he'd planned to do all day. He'd paid her with a gift. Would she be a whore and give herself to him in trade?

Trace slipped his hand beneath the lace edge of her frilly camisole and touched her bare skin. She shivered but didn't pull away. He ventured a little further until his hand covered her ample bosom, the nipple hard in his palm. Dolly even moved her body some, so he could move his hand to the other bosom. He brushed the hard little mound with his calloused finger and she moaned with what Trace thought was pleasure. Her fingers dug into his shoulders and her kiss became more ardent.

Dolly was certainly liking this. Trace broke away from her mouth and kissed down her cheek to her neck. She tasted salty from sweat but had the sweet taste of a woman's desire. He had to taste one of those nipples and pushed the camisole up over the firm mounds of her bosom, arched her back some, and bent to take one of her nipples into his mouth. She gasped with pleasure and relaxed in his arms.

"I think I love you, Trace," she whispered.

Those words brought him to his senses. He pushed Dolly away. Her creamy naked bosoms glowed in the lamplight and he could see his saliva glistening on the hard nipple he'd been suckling. His cock throbbed, and he wanted nothing more than to feel it inside her, but he couldn't go any further.

Dolly yanked her camisole back down into place with tears in her eyes. Were they tears of shame for acting the whore with him or tears of sadness because he hadn't responded to her pronouncement of love for him?

"I'm sorry, Dolly," he said and stormed out of the cabin.

The throbbing between her thighs had abated some when she set the bolt of pretty fabric aside, blew out the lamp, and crawled into the bed, but her tears hadn't. Had she offended Trace by telling him she thought she was in love with him? He doesn't want a whore and she was certainly a whore now.

Dolly didn't understand. In all the novels, if the girl's body reacted the way hers had been reacting to Trace's kisses and touches, it meant they were in love. Her body hadn't reacted like that to Davis, the sheriff, or the Irishman when they'd touched her. Her nipples hadn't throbbed with pleasure neither had the mound of flesh above her cunny. That was only supposed to happen when the woman was in love with the man.

Dolly wept into the pillow. Men must be different from women. She supposed men must be able to take pleasure in a woman without being in love with them, but a woman could only feel pleasure when she loved the man. Was that fair? For the first time in a very long time, Dolly wished her mama was there to explain things to her.

Between fits of weeping and wondering, Dolly had a very long night. Dolly promised herself she wouldn't kiss the man again. He'd only think less of her if she did and feel free to put his hands upon her body. Just thinking about his kisses and his work-rough hands upon her bare skin made Dolly shiver. She'd wanted him to touch her. His mouth upon her bosom had sent waves of pleasure surging through her. Dolly had never experienced anything like it. She'd read about it in her novels but had never thought to experience it for herself.

With tears threatening her eyes again, she remembered the look of shame and disgust on Trace's face before he ran out of the cabin. She didn't suppose she'd ever experience it again. Men were such a bother. They did nothing but cause grief. Why did a woman need one in her life? To do the heavy chores? Dolly had been doing heavy chores around the house for years. She'd spaded up the garden patch every spring and planted it. She'd chopped the wood for the stove. She'd even built the new chicken coop when the old one had finally fallen down.

Dolly had spent the day thinking on what Trace had said about her brother. She'd only been fourteen when her parents had been killed in a buggy accident and in her grief, had never thought much about where the money Martin had spent on things from the mercantile had come from. Her father had owned and worked at the livery in town and Martin had worked there too, but had sold it soon after their parents' deaths, using the excuse that he needed to stay home to care for his little sister. In reality, Dolly had been the one doing the caring for.

Martin immediately began treating Dolly the way their father had treated their poor mother. He called her names and beat her when she didn't do something exactly to his liking. And he drank. The beatings and the yelling were the worst when Martin drank. Over the years, the drinking got worse and the abuse got worse. Dolly had endured it because Martin told her it was all her fault. Daddy and Mama had been out in the buggy that day to buy her a silly dress for a dance she wanted to attend. They were dead because of her and Martin couldn't move away from Concho because he'd been forced to stay and take care of her.

Dolly saw the bolt of cloth and dashed the tears from her face. She was tired of thinking about the men in her miserable life. She wasn't a little girl anymore and it was time for her to start thinking about herself. She'd make a new dress and go to Phoenix or Flagstaff. There had to be something she could do in one of those cities.

Dolly drifted off to sleep with a spark of hope in her heart for a new life.

10

Dolly woke to the sound of someone in the kitchen and bolted upright in the bed.

Trace stood at the stove, forking bacon onto a plate. "Sorry if I woke ya," he said, without turning his head to look at her.

Without speaking to the burly man, Dolly wrapped herself in the thin quilt and went outside barefoot to use the outhouse. The morning air was crisp and cool. Though June, the temperatures up on the mountain were a good twenty degrees cooler than down in Concho. Up here it felt more like April than June.

When she returned to the cabin, Trace sat in his chair on the porch with a plate of food on his lap and a cup of coffee in his hand. "Mr. Snydergaard and maybe his wife will be by sometime this morning, so you'd best keep to the house … dressed as you are and all."

Heat flared in her cheeks at Trace's words and she jerked her head around to glare at the man. "Don't worry," Dolly said, choking back a sob, "the whore will keep out of sight while your friends are here." She stormed inside, slamming the door behind her.

Dressed as she was, huh? Dolly jerked open the wardrobe and pulled out the dress she'd sat in that same chair mending the day before. She'd had to stitch back a sleeve, mend a long rip in the skirt, tack down some lace on the collar, and re-attach the skirt where it had torn away from the bodice. One of the buttons had been lost about midway down and Dolly had replaced it with the one at the collar. She could use her little cameo to secure it there. Other than the faded brown patches where the blood hadn't completely washed out, the dress was as good as new.

Dolly washed her tear-streaked face, put on the dress, and brushed out her hair. She found the plate of food Trace had left for her on the warming rack and took it to the table with a cup of coffee. As she ate the bacon and scrambled eggs, Dolly resolved not to allow the man's words to bother her any longer. After stepping out to collect Trace's empty dishes from the porch, she put water on the stove and mixed up some yeast for bread.

When Dolly heard a wagon out front and men's voices, she pushed the curtain aside, stepping away to stay out of sight. She peeked out to see Trace with a fragile looking gray-headed man unloading things from a buckboard. Dolly didn't see a woman and returned to the kitchen where she intended to cut out the new dress. She'd been thrilled the day before to find Lucy's sewing basket filled with threads of assorted colors, buttons, pins, shears, and bits of lace. It was everything she'd need to put together a new dress.

Dolly had been making her dresses for the past ten years and no longer need a pattern. With the bit of chalk she found in Lucy's kit, she could sketch her pattern onto the fabric and cut it out.

She had half the dress cut out when Trace walked in with a metal can of milk. "This is fresh from this morning's milking," he told her. "I'll take it down to the cellar after I dip out a bit for today's use." She watched him dip out a few ladles of the rich white liquid into a small bowl and set it on the dry sink, and then leave.

Dolly didn't speak but thought it would be nice to have milk for her biscuits and potatoes. She wondered if she should even bother cooking for Trace but saw the plate he'd left food in for her that morning and decided she should.

A little later he returned with a wooden crate in his arms. "Come see what else Mr. Snydergaard has brought."

Dolly put down the scissors and walked over to glance into the box. Soft yellow chicks cheeped at one another on a bed of straw at the bottom. She smiled, bent, and lifted one of the warm fuzzy creatures to her face. "They're so sweet."

"They won't be layin' for a while yet," Trace said with a grin, but when they do, we'll have a good supply of eggs I won't have to haul from Vernon and worry about breakin' before I get 'em home."

She smiled as she nuzzled the chick. "I know we'll need to keep them in here for a while, but where do you plan to put them once they've begun to feather?"

Trace smiled. "Fredrick brought me enough boards and wire to build a nice coop off the back of the stable. I'll build a little brooder box to put them in between the time they're too big for this crate and can be let out onto the ground to scratch for themselves without the worry of critters getting' 'em."

It was obvious to Dolly that Trace was familiar with chickens. "I'll get them some water and some of that cornmeal," she said as she hurried off to the kitchen.

Dolly found two lids to Mason jars. She filled one with water and the other with the ground corn, took them back to the crate, and nestled them into the straw. It wasn't long before the chicks gathered around both, eating and drinking their fill.

Dolly knew she'd need to keep a close watch on them for a few days. If a chick got wet and took a chill, it would die in a matter of hours. She'd have to make certain they all stayed dry and warm.

Trace stared at her. "I see you got that dress all fixed up. I thought for certain, it was a lost cause."

Dolly shrugged. "Nothing that a needle and thread couldn't put back together in a couple of hours." She still found it difficult to look the man in the eyes. She thought the same was true for him.

"I'll probably have enough left on this bolt to make you a shirt, if you want one." She knew he only had one other hanging in the wardrobe. "You're a lot bigger than Martin," Dolly said, "so I'll need to use that cloth tape in Lucy's kit to take some measurements." She gave him a quick glance. "If you want one, that is."

Trace stared at the flowery fabric on the table and grinned. "I fear that's a might girly for a man my size."

"Oh," Dolly said with her face falling a bit, "sure."

"I've gotta get back out there," Trace said. "Fredrick brought me some seed and plant slips I want to get into the ground before nightfall."

He must be planning to stay up here for a spell if he was getting chicks to raise for eggs and planting a garden. She wondered what he planned to do with her.

Dolly returned to the kitchen where her loaves of bread had risen above the top of the pans. She basted them with some bacon fat as she was too low on butter and slid them into the hot oven. They'd have fresh bread with their supper tonight.

While her bread baked, Dolly finished cutting out her new dress. She'd settled on chicken for supper and went down to the cellar for one of the smoked hens Trace had stored there. The dark cellar was cool and smelled of damp earth. She saw the pile of old, sprouting potatoes in the bin and piled them into a basket along with the smoked chicken.

Back inside the house, Dolly cut up the potatoes into chunks with each one sprouting a single eye up toward sunlight. Dolly smelled her bread and cracked open the oven door to see two shiny brown loaves. She pulled them out and set them on the rack to cool.

Dolly cut some slices off the fresh bread and slathered them with butter. She gobbled down the heel before she carried the basket and a plate of fresh bread out to where Trace cut furrows with a push-plow into the loose, loamy soil of the garden area. She handed Trace the plate and then picked up the hoe, leaning beside a tree. "Where do you plan to put the potatoes?"

"Along that fence there," he said as he bit into a slice of the bread and pointed a dirty finger to a spot next to a row of green cabbage slips already in the ground.

Dolly took the hoe and began heaping the soil into a long mound. She took no mind of the soil accumulating on the hem of her dress. It had once been her best Sunday dress, but Dolly knew it, like she, would never see the inside of a church again. It was an everyday work dress now.

※

Trace had been flustered with the young woman when he'd come into the cabin that morning at daybreak to find her still sleeping. Maybe Martin had been right when Trace had heard him calling Dolly a lazy cow all those times. He didn't know how he could have been so wrong about her all these years.

He'd been even more flustered with her when she'd refused to speak to him that morning. She'd been the one who'd kissed him. She hadn't fussed when he'd put his hands on her. She's the one who'd acted the whore. Why hadn't she expected to be treated like one? Had she really expected him to reply to her ridiculous declaration of love? What man could love a whore?

He'd chided her about her clothes and had felt badly about it when he'd returned to the house to find her in the repaired dress. He'd chided himself when his cock had begun to stiffen and throb at the sight of her. No woman had excited him that way since Lucy and his Lucy had been no whore.

Trace had been happy to see Dolly's reaction to the chicks and hear she knew how to care for them at this stage of their lives. He knew she'd had a coop of chickens in the back yard in Concho and seriously doubted her useless brother had ever lifted a hand to care for them. Dolly was the only person in that house Trace had ever seen doing any chores. He chided himself again for thinking her lazy.

The plate of warm yeasty bread had been a surprise. He'd been even more surprised when Dolly picked up the hoe, mounded up a row of soil, and then got to her knees to plant the chunks of potatoes she'd brought out unbidden from the cellar and made ready to plant.

At the end of the row, Trace helped Dolly to her feet. "Thanks for the bread. It was really good."

"Thank you," Dolly replied while brushing off her skirt without looking at him. "I made two loaves."

"You really didn't have to do that," he said, nodding to the mounded row.

Dolly shrugged. "I was in the cellar getting a chicken for supper and saw the old potatoes and knew they needed to get into the ground before they rotted."

Trace reached for her hand, but Dolly pulled it away. "I just wanted to say how sorry I am about the way I acted last night, Dolly." He paused and reached for her hand again.

"It's all right, Trace," she said putting her hand into the other, so he couldn't have it. "I know what you think about me and I can't say as I blame you." She walked over and propped the hoe back where she'd found it. "I'll have supper ready for you later."

Trace watched her walk back to the cabin. He furrowed his brow in frustration and shook his head. He'd never understand women. Had she expected him to fall down on his knees and beg her forgiveness? Wasn't his apology good enough? He'd tried to be sincere.

Trace grumbled in his head as he finished planting peas, green beans, sweet corn, squash, melons, cucumbers, and yams. He wished Fredrick had brought peppers, but he'd said he and the wife didn't eat them. Trace studied the tidy rows and smiled. If everything thrived, this garden would feed them for the summer and into the winter if Dolly canned the way Lucy had. Trace knew she did, because he'd seen her garden in the back yard and watched her tend it, hoeing and pulling weeds in the hot sun while Martin was nowhere to be seen.

The supper that night of chicken and dumplings was delicious, but strained with little conversation. Trace didn't know what she expected him to say and he refused to apologize for something he didn't think he needed to apologize for. She was the one who'd kissed him. She was the one who hadn't pulled away when he'd touched her and suckled her bosoms. She should be apologizing to him for leading him on to think there might be more.

By the time he'd filled his belly, Trace was so riled at the woman again that he pushed his plate aside without thanking her for another fine meal and stomped out of the cabin. Was this what it was going to be like between them now?

Trace had always hated it when he and Lucy had a row. It had usually been his fault and after he'd apologized they'd make love and everything would be right with the world again. He couldn't expect that with Dolly.

Should he have made mention of what she'd said to him the night before about thinking she was in love with him? How the hell did she expect him to address that? Was he supposed to tell her he loved her too? Did he? He'd always felt an attraction to the pretty redhead. He'd even asked Martin to court her, but he hadn't been willing to part with the hundred dollars Martin wanted as a bride-price for his sister.

It gnawed at Trace's gut that had he paid Martin and taken the girl as his wife, none of this would have happened to her and she might have even borne him children already. Trace fed the horses and then retired to his blankets.

He'd never understand the workin' of a woman's mind if he lived to be a hundred.

***

The Irishman had his wagon parked outside Fort Whipple near the Arizona Territorial Capitol of Prescott. Business had been brisk. The soldiers had just been paid and had money in their pockets for the whiskey and cunny he had in plenty to offer.

They'd recently acquired a young girl they'd found wandering alone near a small farmstead. His cock still throbbed from listening to her scream and beg. He'd taken Davis's lead and offered the virgin girl's cunny to the highest bidder and told the winning bidder to have his way with her in every hole to break her in. The big uniformed officer had paid an extra five dollars for one of his big friends to join in on the training. When they'd finished with her, the girl had to take on ten more and by the end of the night, she was beaten and battered, but a proper whore. He and Pauly had taken turns with her the way he and that sheriff had taken the redhead and he'd filled the girl's mouth twice with his seed.

"Where to from here, boss?" Pauly asked as he cleaned the girl from his withered cock.

"East," the Irishman told him. "They still haven't heard from Davis in San Francisco." He upended his bottle of fine Irish whiskey and waited for the smooth amber liquid to warm his belly. "We'll hit the forts between here and Flagstaff and then backtrack to where we saw him last with that redhead."

Pauly grinned through his bushy, dark beard and squeezed his soft cock. "I'm ready to give that one's cunny a good pokin' if Davis has relieved her of that valuable maidenhood already."

"Me thoughts exactly, boyo," the Irishman said with a loud drunken chuckle.

11

The two weeks following the planting of the garden were blissful and hinted at a future Dolly never thought possible.

It took them three days to build the new chicken coop onto the rear of the small stable. Dolly had been surprised at Trace's skills with a hammer and saw. He planted cedar posts into the ground and Dolly helped him to stretch wire to keep the chickens in and the critters out of the new coop. He built nesting boxes in the small enclosed spaces where the hens would someday lay their eggs and set up branches for roosts. Trace also built a four-foot by four-foot enclosed box up on legs as a brooder pen for the chicks to go into as they transitioned from the crate in the house to running loose in the coop outside.

The garden sprouted peas, beans, and even a few of the potatoes Dolly had planted as the sun warmed the rich soil. She looked forward to seeing the rows filled with green blooming plants in the upcoming weeks and she wondered at the condition of her poor garden down in Concho. Had Martin been tending to it? Sadly, Dolly suspected he hadn't and that weeds had taken over. She worried over her chickens too. Had he bothered to feed and water them or collect the eggs?

The day after she'd finished her dress, Trace took her on her first trip into Vernon. He'd saddled the sheriff's gray mare for her to ride and told her the animal's name was either Bess or Tess. He couldn't recall for certain. Dolly decided she looked more like a Bess and settled on that.

Wearing her new dress and with her red hair tied back in a kerchief she'd made with the same fabric, they set out for the tiny settlement. Dolly, never having learned to ride side-saddle, rode with her skirts hiked up astraddle the horse.

"I suppose I should make myself a split riding skirt," she told Trace. "I've seen pictures of them in periodicals and they look easy enough to make."

Trace stared at her with a brow cocked in confusion and Dolly grinned. "It's a skirt made like wide trousers, so I could ride without showing my ankles."

"Oh," he said and nodded, though Dolly suspected he still didn't understand.

The soft breeze smelled of pines and Dolly enjoyed the green everywhere. Cedars, grass, and wild flowers grew around Concho in the high desert below, but it was still desert and more brown than green most of the year. Up here on the mountain, it was a riot of green and full of life.

She saw colorful butterflies and birds in the air, squirrels running up the broad trunks of the pines, and deer and elk in the grassy meadows they passed by. Snow-fed streams and creeks rushed past them into lakes.

"Do you like to fish?" Dolly asked Trace as they came upon one of the bodies of water trapped in a deep valley along the trail.

"When I've got the time," he said with a grin. "Do you know how to cook trout? It's about all there are in the lakes up here."

"My daddy loved his trout." Dolly said with a sad smile. "Of course, I can cook trout."

Trace nodded. "I'll keep that in mind."

They came upon a lush farmstead with cows grazing in a green field before a tall, whitewashed farmhouse and barns. "That's the Snydergaard place," Trace told her as he waved at on old woman tossing grain to chickens in the yard. "That's Helga, Fredrick's wife. Most folks up here regard her as a witch."

"Why?" Dolly asked as she watched the stooped old woman dressed in black like a widow.

Trace shrugged his broad shoulders. "She's a bit odd and makes potions and such she calls medicine from the old country."

"Where is she from?"

"Norway, I think" Fredrick said. "They speak English with an accent."

"All of our families came to this country from somewhere," Dolly said. "Only the Indians can say they're actually from here. To them, we all speak with an accent."

Trace chuckled. "I guess you're right. I never thought on it like that before." He opened his canteen and took a swallow. "Where are your people from, Dolly? I think my mama said Daddy's hailed from Scotland and her's from Sweden."

"The Stroud family came over from England before the Revolution and settled in Kentucky to farm, but I think my mama's people came over from Scotland." Dolly touched her hair. "She said it's where this came from. Her grandmother was a redhead too."

"A good many Scottish folks fled to America during their war with England, called The Uprising."

His knowledge of history impressed Dolly. "I suppose your reddish hair came from your Scottish roots as well."

Trace grinned. "I'd wager the two of us could fill this mountain with a passel of redheaded little Scotsmen."

Dolly's eyes went wide at the comment. Had he been thinking about having children with her? Dolly doubted that. He hadn't made any more advances toward her and she'd stayed clear of him. They'd worked on the coop together and taken their meals together but hadn't so much as touched since that night when she'd lost her head and kissed him.

They rode on in uncomfortable silence to Vernon. The little settlement wasn't much to speak of, with the big clapboard building Trace told her was the mercantile, a Town Hall, and a few other buildings.

A few horses were tied outside another building Trace told her was a saloon and dining hall for the loggers. He told her they could eat there before returning home if she didn't mind that it was a saloon.

Dolly shrugged. Why should she mind eating in a saloon? She was a whore now. Weren't whores supposed to feel at home in saloons?

They were met inside by a thin, woman of middle years with her graying hair pulled up into a severe bun on the top of her head. She greeted them with tin cups filled with cool, sweet water.

The water felt good on Dolly's tongue after the long ride and she thanked the woman who stood, studying Dolly.

"And who might this pretty, young thing be, Trace?" the woman asked with a grin.

Dolly watched his red face turn redder as he tried to think. "Vivian, this is Dolly. She's my … eh … She's my new wife."

Dolly's mouth fell open. His wife? "Dolly," Trace said uneasily, staring at her. "This is Vivian Sanders. She and her husband, Don, own the mercantile."

"Your wife?" the woman gasped, taking Dolly into her arms. "Trace never hinted at having a new wife when he was in here before." She lifted the skirt of Dolly's dress and grinned. "Now I know why he was pickin' through my bolts the last time he was in here." The woman tugged Dolly through the store to a table piled high with bolts of fabric. "I just got some new stock in from Denver."

Vivian turned to Trace, who followed along behind. "A woman can't have too much fabric, you know, especially when she might have youngins coming along any time."

She patted Dolly's belly and then pulled the skirt away from Dolly's body to admire it. "You did an excellent job on this, young lady. I can't sew worth a lick. My mother used to tell me I'd better marry a rich man who could afford a seamstress for me because I was all thumbs with a needle in my hand." She laughed as she pulled out a bolt of green plaid and held it up to Trace. "Your husband could do with a new shirt or two," Vivian said with a giggle. "I bet that's the same one he's worn into my store the last three times he's been in here."

By the time they left the store with the list of things they'd come for, they also had four additional bolts of fabric, the buttons for Trace's two new shirts and the lace and ribbon to trim new underthings and a night dress for Dolly.

"Take good care of that man, Dolly," Vivian whispered to her as Trace secured their purchases to the horses, "he's as good as they come around here."

"I know," Dolly said as she watched the handsome man securing the ungainly stack of fabric behind her saddle. "I know."

Trace walked back and took Dolly's hand. "Shall we get a bite of lunch before headin' home?"

"I suppose," she said before turning to the proprietress. "Thank you, so much, ma'am. It was real nice meeting you."

Vivian Sanders smiled. "It's been a pleasure meeting you as well, Mrs. Anderson. I look forward to seeing your handsome husband in one of those new shirts very soon—perhaps at the Summer Social."

Trace gave her hand a slight tug toward the horses. "We'll think on it, Mrs. Sanders, but it's a long ride from the cabin to come into Vernon for a dance." He grinned. "I can't dance anyhow. I'd step on my poor Dolly's toes and she wouldn't be able to walk afterward."

"Well," Vivian sighed with a wink and a grin at Dolly, "the next time you're in for supplies, then."

They waved and led the horses toward the saloon. "She's not gonna be seein' me for a while." He glanced at the pile of fabric tied behind Dolly's saddle and shook his head. "I'd reckon that woman could sell water to a drownin' man."

"She does have a way about her, but I'd imagine she was just being extra nice to your new bride."

"Yah," Trace coughed, "about that. I reckon I should have warned you first."

Dolly gave him a dismissive wave. "I understand. You certainly couldn't have it look like you'd moved a whore into your house up here. What would people think?"

Trace removed his hat and ran a hand through his wavy,

reddish-brown hair that Dolly noticed was curling up at his collar. He needed a haircut. He took Bess's reigns from Dolly and tied them to the rail outside the saloon. "Let's get something to fill our bellies before heading home. It'll be too late for you to cook once we get there and you'll be tired from ridin'."

Dolly didn't know what to expect. She'd never been in a saloon before. Martin frequented them, but Dolly had been warned against ever entering one in Sunday School, as they were places of sin and sloth where men were tempted with alcohol, gambling, and evil women of low repute.

Dolly supposed she was one of those women now and sighed as she stepped inside the building behind Trace. The room smelled of stale tobacco, food, and unwashed, sweaty men. A few sat at the tables, eating and looked up from their plates to view the newcomers.

The place looked like one of the few restaurants Dolly had ever visited, and she relaxed a little. They took seats and a woman came toward their table dressed in a colorful dress with a very low-cut neckline, revealing the tops of her mounded bosoms. Dolly felt her cheeks flushing and looked away from the woman.

"What can I get for you folks?"

"What's the special in the kitchen today?" Trace asked.

"Elk stew over white rice," she said. "That with a sarsaparilla or a beer is fifteen cents."

"Sounds good," Trace told the woman. "My wife and I will each have that with sarsaparillas, please."

Dolly smiled. She supposed he was going to keep up the pretense for the time being. It wasn't so bad, pretending to be Trace's wife. Lord knows, she'd thought about being just that many times over the past couple of years. She'd fantasized about him barging into the house and taking her away from Martin to live across the street with him in the house he'd once shared with Lucy.

The woman returned with two mugs filled with foamy brown liquid. Trace picked his up and swallowed a mouth full. Dolly did the same, with hesitation. She'd never had sarsaparilla and didn't know if it was alcoholic. She'd never consumed alcohol either. Silky sweetness filled Dolly's mouth and she swallowed with delight until Trace stopped her by pulling the mug away from her mouth.

"Don't founder yourself on the first mug, girl," he scolded with a grin on his lips. "Have you never tasted sarsaparilla before?"

Dolly shook her head with her cheeks flushing. "No, I've never had it before. It's good."

Trace shook his head with a frown on his face. "Martin should be horse-whipped for treatin' you the way he did and denyin' you the things every other young person out there has enjoyed." He reached across the table and took Dolly's hand again. "I'm so sorry for not meetin' his bride-price when he asked it of me. Things would have been so much different for the both of us if I had."

Dolly's mouth fell open and her eyes went wide. What did he mean? What bride-price? Martin had been asking a bride-price for her?

"You didn't know I'd asked Martin to pay court to you?"

"No," Dolly said with a shake of her head as her heart pounded in her chest. Trace had wanted to court her? Why hadn't Martin told her? "I never knew. When?"

"A few months after Lucy died," he said, "just before I asked you to stop comin' by to help around the house."

"Martin refused to let you court me?"

Trace rolled his eyes and let out a long sigh. "He said he'd tell me like he'd told all the other's who'd called to court you, that I'd have to pay him the bride-price of a hundred dollars first."

Dolly choked in surprise. A hundred dollars? There had been others? "What others?" she gasped and coughed.

"The son-of-a-bitch never told you other young men had come to ask to court you and he'd turned them away because they couldn't pay his ridiculous bride-price?"

"Why would anybody pay a bride-price before he knew if he wanted the girl for his wife yet?"

"Because your brother is a scoundrel who assumed the man courting you would get you into bed and sample the wares first."

The woman brought their food and set it on the table in front of them, but Dolly had suddenly lost her appetite. How could Martin have done that to her? Tears of rage at her brother filled Dolly's eyes. She could have been married by now with a home and children.

"I didn't mean to upset you, Dolly," Trace said, taking her hand again. "I should have paid Martin's price, Dolly, and taken you out of that house a long time ago. I'm so sorry."

Dolly loosed her hand from his and put it in her lap. "I'm not mad at you, Trace, but I'm furious with Martin." She trembled with rage as she shook her head. "He always said no men in town wanted to court me because I was lazy and homely. I was destined to be an old maid our parents had shackled him with." She squeezed her eyes shut against the tears that wanted to fall. "How could he have done that to me?"

"Because Martin Stroud is a greedy, lazy bastard who wanted to keep you all to himself to keep house and cook for him."

"But why?" Dolly demanded in a voice that drew attention from the other people in the room.

"Because every other woman on the damned rim could see him for what he is and wouldn't give him the time of day," Trace explained, telling Dolly the hard truth about her brother she'd never been willing to see for herself. "He's a lazy, greedy drunkard who had a woman at home to take care of his house, cook for him, and do his laundry. Why would he give that up and have to tend for himself without you?"

"Well, he has to tend for himself now," Dolly spat. "He was more than willing to hand me over to be humiliated and made a whore by Davis in my own home for the price of his damned debts."

"Try to eat a little, sweetheart," Trace said in a low, soothing tone, "and let's head home where I'm sure you're eager to start cutting into that pile of fabric out there on Bess."

Dolly picked up the fork in her trembling hand. How could she have been so blind to Martin all these years? Trace was right about her brother and Dolly felt like a damned fool. She put a chunk of savory elk into her mouth and chewed, but it had no flavor to her. Dolly forced herself to take a few more bites, but the food rested like lead shot in her stomach and threatened to come back up the more she thought about what Trace had told her.

Dolly dropped the fork into the plate and pushed herself to her feet. "I'm finished," she mumbled. "I need some air."

As Dolly strode toward the door, a man who resembled her brother grabbed her arm. "Hey, darlin'," he crooned with the smell of whiskey on his breath, "if you're done with the big fella over there," he bent closer, grinning into Dolly's face and filling her nose with his foul breath, "why don't ya come upstairs with me and let me give you a little tickle." Dolly tried to pull her arm from his grasp, but he wouldn't let her go. He shook her. "Don't be such a sour cunny, bitch, or I'll put you on your knees right here and make you suck me in front of everyone."

The memories of Davis and the Irishman flooded into Dolly's head. She didn't intend to be put on her knees by anyone ever again. "That's more like it, darlin'," the man said, "now let's go see what—"

He couldn't finish his disgusting sentence. Dolly had balled up her fist and in a fit of pure rage, drew back and delivered a blow to the man's mouth that sent him reeling across the floor.

"I'm not your darlin' and I'm not your whore, sir," Dolly said to the man on the floor in a calm voice as she rubbed her bruised knuckles, turned, and strolled out of the saloon with Trace close behind.

12

The ride home was unnervingly quiet.

They rode slower with the horses loaded as they were and Trace found it hard to look at Dolly as they rode. He'd been on his way to her side when she'd struck the man and sent him floundering to the saloon floor. He wanted to talk to Dolly about what had happened, but she wouldn't reply in more than one word sentences, so he finally gave up trying. He'd simply never fathom women. Was she mad at him for not running to her rescue from the man or was she still upset with him for what she'd heard from him about Martin? The woman was as pig-headed as a mule when it came to her damned brother and Trace was getting tired of it.

"I'm sorry you had to hear about it from me," Trace said as they neared the Snydergaard place.

Dolly turned. "Had to hear what? That the brother I loved, and thought loved me only really cared about the work he could get out of me, and eventually a bride-price?"

Trace had never heard such utter sourness come from Dolly's mouth. It cut him to the quick to hear it, but he was glad to hear she'd finally seen the bastard for what he was. "You don't ever need to go back to him, Dolly. You're free of him now."

"You really mean I can never go back to my home now. I can never go back to my life in Concho or my home." She narrowed her eyes and scowled at Trace. "I'm free of Martin, but free to do what?" Tears slipped out of her eyes to slide down her sun-reddened cheeks. "I'm free to be a whore now, is what you mean."

Trace watched Dolly swipe the tears away. "Do you want me to be your wife now, Trace?" she demanded. "That bastard back there at the saloon took me for a whore and he didn't even know me. I know you take me for a whore now too, after what you saw."

Trace couldn't make any words come from his mouth in reply. Dolly stared at him for a minute with the tears glistening on her cheeks and brimming in her sad blue eyes. "I'll go on home, so you can stop at your friend's without lying to him about the whore who lives in your house now." She kicked at the mare, urging Bess toward the cabin with the bolts of fabric swaying on the animal's rump.

"Oh, for Christ's sake," Trace muttered in frustration and turned his mount into the lane leading up to Helga and Fredrick's farmhouse.

"Who was that fine looking piece of woman flesh, young Trace?" Fredrick asked with a grin on his weathered old face.

"My wife, Dolly," Trace said without reservation.

The old man raised a white brow. "So, that's the reason you've been building chicken coops and planting a garden like before you lost Miss Lucy and the babe." He took off his wide-brimmed straw hat and wiped the sweat from the thinning white hair on his head. "Why didn't you mention her before? I'd have been proud to meet her."

Trace didn't know how to explain things to the man he look at as a father figure. He got down from his horse and let it all out. He told Fredrick about what had happened to Dolly and why. Trace told him he'd shot at the foul sheriff, but he couldn't bring himself to admit he'd killed the man. He told Fredrick about Dolly's kiss and her exclamation of love and his inability to deal with it.

Fredrick scratched his bearded chin. "How do you feel about her, boy? You called her your wife. Is that the way you see her?"

Trace leaned against his horse and sighed. "I asked to court her once," he admitted, "but didn't want to meet her brother's ridiculous bride-price."

The old man smiled, "So you wanted the pudding, but didn't want to pay the cook?"

"That's not what I said."

"That's exactly what you said, boy."

Trace took off his hat and ran a hand through his thick wiry hair. "I don't know what I should do now, Fredrick. I can't take her back down to her brother in Concho. She'd never be accepted back there. The women in town would label her a whore and run her out of town and the men … well the men would …" Trace hesitated, "the men would just be men and make her life hell after what happened. She can't go back there."

The old man poked his gnarled index finger into Trace's broad chest. "But what do you want?"

Trace released a long breath and stared into the man's eyes. "I want her, Fredrick. I want Dolly."

"Have you told her that?" Trace made no reply. "Then get up off your bull-headed behind and go tell the girl."

"But we can't live together in sin," Trace objected.

Frederick snorted. "The old woman and me have lived together for over forty years now and we never went before no preacher. Her father in Norway wanted another man for her." He grinned. "But Helga wanted me and we ran off together. She bore me nine children of which only three lived to adulthood. She and they carry my name, but it's only because it's what we decided and not some church men." He shook his head and put his hand on his chest. "It's what is in here that counts, boy, not what's on some piece of paper somewhere."

Trace's mouth fell open. "I'd never have known."

"My point exactly, boy. The way you choose to live is between you and the girl. It's nobody else's concern. Treat her like a wife, and everyone will say she's your wife because she is your wife." Fredrick poked Trace's chest again. "It's what's in here that makes her your wife and you her husband, not words spoken by some man in a black suit or scribbling on a piece of paper."

"But what do I do when people call her a whore?" Trace mumbled.

The old man snorted and grinned at the younger man. "The same thing I do when they call my Helga a witch," he said. "Duck and hope I can get out of her way quick enough."

Trace laughed. "Thanks, Fredrick. I needed to talk to someone before my head exploded."

"Get on that horse, boy and get on down the road. Tell that young woman how you feel before she gets it into her head to get on her horse and find a man who will."

"I'll do that." Trace swung his leg up over the saddle, reached into his pocket and pulled out a silver coin to hand down to the old man. "Here's a dollar for more milk and that side of beef we talked about. Are you still plannin' to butcher sometime soon?"

"That, I am. Are you still thinking about moving your leather works up here and building a shop?"

Trace smiled. "If you still have a mind to supply me with the leather I'll need."

Fredrick nodded. "I talked to my oldest boy and he's building up his tannery. He thinks we can keep you supplied."

"That's good to know. I intend to talk to Dolly about it tonight." Trace used his boots to nudge his mare forward. "I'll be seein' ya tomorrow, then with the milk."

"You will," Frederick called after the younger man. "And I may bring the old witch along with me to meet your young misses."

Trace smiled and shook his head as he urged his mare back onto the trail. Fredrick had given him a lot to think about. The last time they'd spoken, Trace had discussed moving his saddlery shop up the mountain with the old man. Fredrick's son, Lars, ran a small tannery and his daughter's husband worked at a sawmill. Trace could get the materials he'd need, and Mrs. Sanders had assured him she would take his goods in trade.

He ambled toward home in good spirits. It was high time he spoke to Dolly about the future—their future together.

By the time Dolly arrived back at the cabin, her tears had left trails through the dust on her sunburned cheeks. The late afternoon sun dappled the ground through the branches of the tall pines. She smelled rain and hoped the temperatures didn't dip too low. Snow in June on the mountain wasn't unheard of.

Her mouth was dry, and she drank from the dipper in the water bucket when she went inside. When Dolly saw her face in the small mirror above the washbasin, she groaned. Her eyes were swollen from crying and her face smeared with trail dust turned to mud.

"Well, aren't you a mess," Dolly said to her reflection.

She pulled off the kerchief from her head and scratched her sweaty scalp before pouring some water into the basin and washing her face. She heard the chicks making a fuss in their crate and Dolly peeked in to see they'd upended both their food and water. Two of them had jumped to the top of the crate and sat looking around defiantly from their new roosting spot. They'd all be hopping up there soon and then be out into the room.

"I think you all are about ready to move out of the parlor and into the coop outside," she said as she reached down to retrieve the empty lids to carry into the kitchen and refill.

Dolly was proud that she hadn't lost one of the dozen chicks since taking charge of them, though their smell had become overpowering in the confined space and the constant cheeping got on her nerves some.

She returned the filled food and water containers and went out to unburden her horse. She untied the bolts of fabric and carried them inside to the table. Dolly looked forward to cutting and sewing the new garments. She thought about the unfinished shirt on her sewing basket at Martin's and sighed, knowing it would never be finished now.

"Come on, Bess, let's get you back to the stable and take this saddle off. I know you must be tired too." Dolly led the mare to her stall in the quiet stable, unbuckled the saddle, and slid it off the gray mare's back. After dropping it over a bench, Dolly pulled off the blanket and rubbed Bess down before using the curry comb on her.

She filled the bins with feed and carried water from the creek to fill the troughs. Dolly checked the saddlebags and smiled when she saw a parcel tucked inside one of them. She couldn't recall what it could have been.

When she got back inside, Dolly pulled away the paper to find a large bundle of narrow lace, several cards with white buttons attached to them — some sized for men's shirts and some tiny for a woman's camisole, a card of hooks and eyes, and an assortment of satin ribbons to match the colors in the fabrics. When had Mrs. Sanders put all of this together? Had Trace asked her to do it? Tears sprang to Dolly's eyes at the thoughtfulness.

Suspecting Trace would be as hungry as she was when he got home, Dolly took a plate and sharp knife to the smokehouse and sliced off some of the salty ham. She would warm it and slice up one of the loaves she'd made a few days ago for a light meal. She'd found a crock of sweet pickles in the cellar that would be good with the ham and bread.

Before setting the fabric aside, Dolly took some time to examine it. She was surprised to find Mrs. Sanders had added in some short remnants from other bolts of solid and contrasting fabrics Dolly could use for yokes, collars, and cuffs. Her head buzzed with possibilities. She longed to make one of the fancy frilled bustled gowns she'd seen in a periodical, but those weren't dresses one wore to mop floors or weed a garden in. She'd stick with simple yoked blouses and skirts with a wide ruffle at the bottom and maybe a bit of lace at the collar.

Trace walked in to find her at the table fingering the lace and ribbons she'd found in the saddlebag. He put the crates of supplies he carried in his arms on the dry sink.

"Lucy always needed those extra frilly bits for her sewin'," he said and kissed the top of Dolly's head. "You didn't need to feed and water the horses. I would have done that."

Dolly felt a thrill jolt through her body with the touch of his warm lips on her head. She'd longed to feel them on hers again but shut her eyes tightly to push that thought from her head. She wouldn't act the wanton with him again.

"Bess was thirsty, and the troughs were empty," Dolly said with a shrug as she stood to clear the table and went to the crates. "I'll put this all away and get us something to eat."

Trace smiled. "Good. I'm starvin'."

Dolly filled the bin in the pie safe with fresh flour, placed the carefully packed eggs into a bowl, amazed Trace could get them home on the bouncing horse without cracking even one, and stored the bars of soap and chlorine crystals beneath the dry sink. She desperately needed to wash her white underthings.

She glanced at the bolt of white cotton and smiled. It would be nice to have fresh ones to wear.

They sat at the table with their meal of toasted bread, ham, pickles, and water. "I hope this is all right," Dolly said.

Trace had slathered two slices of bread with butter and slapped slices of warm ham and pickles between them. "This is great, Dolly." He bit into the combination and chewed. When he'd finished one, he made another. "Mr. Snydergaard is bringing more milk tomorrow," he told her and grinned. "He's also bringing Helga with him to meet my new wife."

"Oh, my," Dolly said as her face fell. "We need to get those smelly chicks out of here and air this place out if we're going to have company."

Trace took her hand and smiled. "Calm down Mrs. Anderson. Fredrick and Helga are farmers. They're used to having chicks in the parlor."

"You intend to keep up that Mrs. Anderson story?" Dolly asked and took a swallow of water.

"Don't you want to be Mrs. Anderson?"

Dolly's eyes darted around the room. "Of course, I do, Trace, but …"

Trace leapt from his chair with a smile on his face. He yanked Dolly to her feet, wrapped his arms around her slender body, and kissed her hard on the mouth.

As his groin began to stir, Dolly broke away. "Do you really want me to be your wife Trace? Even after …"

He took her head between her hands. "Even after, Dolly. I want us to live together up here as man and wife."

Dolly stepped back, pondering his words. "You want us to live as man and wife, but you don't actually want to make me your wife before a minister in the church?"

"Is that really necessary?" he asked with a furrowed brow. "I want to be with you and I think you want to be with me. Do we need more than that to be man and wife?"

Dolly's lip trembled as she stared at the floor. "I want to be your wife, Trace, and I think I love you, but I don't want to be just your whore. I want to share your life here as well as your bed."

Trace didn't say anything. He pushed past Dolly with her mouth hanging open and stormed out to the stable.

13

Trace wore a scowl on his handsome face when he walked in that morning and Dolly didn't know what to expect.

She had breakfast on the table when Trace came in the cabin that morning and had already moved the chicks to the brooder box in the coop. She wore her new dress and stood at the counter, mixing something up in the stoneware mixing bowl.

"I'm making a cake for your friends," she told Trace with an uneasy smile as he washed his face and shaved.

Trace scowled at the girl in the mirror. "Helga and Fredrick are country people, Dolly. There is no need to put on airs with them."

Dolly's mouth fell open. "I just thought a cake would be nice for your friends, Trace."

She watched him dry his face and drop into his chair at the table where he gobbled down his breakfast and drank his coffee without speaking a word.

What had she done now? Was he mad because she wanted to be a real wife and not just his whore? Dolly didn't intend to allow another man to take advantage of her—not even Trace Anderson. How could he expect that of her?

She put the cake pans in the oven. She planned to make a jam cake with the raspberry jam between two layers of yellow cake and drizzled with a sugar and jam glaze. The cake was nothing fancy, but one Dolly had won high praise for at church socials.

She tidied the kitchen, brushed out her hair again and waited for Trace's guests to arrive. Did she really want to continue with this deception of being Trace's wife when she wasn't? Dolly hated lying. Why couldn't they just be honest? She was a friend from Concho visiting for a while and he was sleeping in the stable while Dolly slept in the house. Men!

Dolly smelled the cake and went to the kitchen to check it. She'd pulled the pans from the oven when she heard the wagon outside and hurried to the porch, nervous and excited to meet Trace's friends and their nearest neighbors. She waved and watched Trace help the old woman down from the wagon.

She wore black, as Dolly had seen her before. She was a stout, buxom woman with her white hair braided and pinned up on her head. The man was thin and gray-headed as well, with a beard cut in the same fashion as Mr. Lincoln's with no mustache.

The old man took a can of milk from the wagon and the woman a heavy basket. She walked toward the cabin with a smile on her face while Trace took the can of milk from the old man and walked with it toward the cellar.

"Hello, young woman," the woman said in greeting with an accent Dolly had never heard before. Trace had told her the couple were Norwegian. Dolly supposed the White Mountains were as close to Norway as they'd find in Arizona.

Dolly stepped off the porch and offered the woman her hand. "I'm Dolly. It's so nice to meet you."

"And I am Helga," she said and handed Dolly the basket she carried. "A little gift in honor of your joining with our dear young Trace."

Dolly took the basket with guilty reservation. How could she in all honesty accept a wedding gift when she wasn't wed? "Thank you," Dolly said. "Would you like to come in? I'm working on a cake."

"Oh, yes, please," Helga said as she hobbled up onto the porch.

DOLLY

"I fear these old bones aren't quite what they used to be." She pronounced her 'th' like a 'z' and her 'w' like a 'v'. Dolly found it exotic and charming.

Dolly led her inside to one of the kitchen chairs. "Would you like a cup of coffee? I just made a fresh pot."

"That would be nice." The old woman stared around the cabin. "This is a very nice little place. I haven't been in here since poor Lucy passed."

Dolly set a cup of coffee on the table. "Sugar or cream?"

"Both if you please." She smiled with a mouth missing several teeth. "I have never become accustomed to drinking it black as you Americans say."

Dolly set the pitcher of milk she'd prepared and the cone of sugar on the table. "I'm going to finish my cake, if you don't mind. The jam goes on easier and soaks in better if the cake is still warm."

Helga gave her a dismissive wave. "Don't let me keep you from your work, child. I will sit here and enjoy the sitting. You don't get to do much of that on a dairy farm. There is milking, tending the animals, processing the milk, and then more milking." Helga giggled. "Fredrick and me have shared a busy life together."

Dolly smiled as she smeared jam onto the layers of warm yellow cake. "I've always found it better to stay busy than idle and bored."

"If that is the case," Helga said with a grin, "Then Trace has married a fine woman." When Dolly didn't make a reply the old woman added. "Don't be worried, girl. Fredrick told me you and Trace never went before a minister to speak the bans any more than he and I did."

Dolly turned her head to stare at the woman with her eyes wide. "You and Fredrick aren't mar…"

"We are as much married as any couple is who've shared a bed together for forty years are married." She smiled her toothless smile and patted her left breast. "We are married in here and that is all that matters."

"Do you have children?"

"I've borne my dear Fredrick nine children," she said with her smile fading. "Three never took a breath once outside my womb before we sailed to this new land, three died of fevers before their fifth summers here in this new world, and of the three that survived, one was taken by Indians and I never saw her again." Helga brushed a hand over her dress. "It is for her sake I wear the grieving clothes."

"I'm so very sorry for all your losses, Helga," Dolly told the old woman as she refilled her cup, thinking about how horrible it must have been to have a living child stolen away never to be seen again. "I lost my parents when I was a girl. They died in a buggy accident and it still hurts to think of them today."

Helga took Dolly's hand in hers. "Thank you, young woman. That is very kind." She released her hand. "Luckily, our remaining son and daughter have gifted my Fredrick and me with six wonderful grandchildren. We are truly blessed, indeed."

Dolly returned to the counter to assemble her cake and mix up jam. water and sugar to drizzle over the top and run down the sides of the sweet marvel. The only thing missing was a few fresh raspberries to decorate the top. Dolly lifted the heavy plate and carried it to the table where Helga smiled in admiration.

"Trace is a lucky man to have found a woman who can cook such marvels for him." The old woman smiled at Dolly as she joined her at the table with her own cup of coffee. "It is a lucky man who finds a woman who can satisfy him in the kitchen as much as she satisfies him in the bedroom."

Dolly felt her cheeks flush. "I know he is happy with my cooking," Dolly said softly, "but I can't comment as to the other. We haven't…"

Helga's old, filmy eyes went wide. "You've not experienced his manhood?" The old woman grinned as she sipped her coffee. "Does one buy a horse without taking it out for a good ride first?"

Dolly's mouth fell open in surprise. She'd never heard such talk from a woman of Helga's age. Perhaps they did things very differently where she came from.

"You will think me an immoral old witch with such talk, like all the others on this mountain," Helga said with a sigh. "Perhaps I am."

"Why would they call you witch?"

Helga shrugged. "Perhaps because I'm foreign, wear only black, and have lost my teeth," she said and grinned. "But they still come to me when their little ones have a cough and need my elderberry syrup or they have aches and pains in their head and want my willow bark tea." She winked. "And the women who've borne too many children already come when they want my wild carrot seeds to keep them from growing heavy again with a child, or my pennyroyal oil to expel the child from their womb when the carrot seed didn't work."

"Oh, my," Dolly gasped. "You'll have to teach me all of that. I've always been curious about medicines and how to make them."

Helga smiled. "They will curse you as a witch, but perhaps you will not lose your teeth and wear black like this old woman and they will hold their tongues." She emptied her cup. "In that basket you will find a wheel of yellow cheese, some of Fredricks amazing sausages, a crock of soft white cheese that would have made a lovely icing for that cake, and some packets of my willow bark tea for when your man has over-worked himself or received an injury, causing him pain."

"Thank you, Helga. I appreciate it very much and I'm sure Trace will too."

The woman got up and hobbled to the window where the men could be heard talking. "Get in here, you two, so we can taste Dolly's beautiful cake."

※

The scowl had left Trace's face by the time he and Fredrick joined the women at the table. Fredrick had a way of lifting his spirits. They'd talked about where to add onto the cabin to build and house his shop, as well as an addition for a bedroom. He couldn't expect Dolly to continue sleeping in what was essentially the kitchen for much longer.

"Look at this beautiful cake Dolly has made to share with us,

Papa," Helga said as Fredrick took a seat at the table. "Isn't it lovely?"

The old man offered his hand to Dolly. "It's as lovely as the lady who baked it."

"Sit down and stop talking like an old flirt," Helga chided her husband. Trace refused to think of them in any other way than husband and wife no matter that they'd never said vows in a church.

Trace patted his stomach. "Dolly's bound and determined to fatten me up like a hog for slaughter."

"Just because she cooks it doesn't require you to eat it," Helga said with a grin.

Trace stuffed a piece of the cake Dolly had cut for him into his mouth and smiled. "How can I not, when it's all so good?"

"You are a lucky man, Trace," Fredrick said as he chewed a bite of the rich, moist cake, "to have found a woman who can create such delights in your kitchen." He winked at Helga and raised his cup of coffee in a salute. "May she delight you as well in your bedroom."

"Papa don't embarrass the girl," Helga chided her grinning husband while raising her cup as well.

Trace took Dolly's hand into his and grinned at her red face. "I am a very lucky man," he said, "I never thought I'd find another woman to settle down with after I lost my Lucy, but now I have Dolly and I couldn't be happier."

His heart warmed to see Dolly's smile. He'd been too hard on her. If she wanted a wedding before a minister, then he'd do what he could to make that happen. They ate their cake, finished off a pot of coffee and shared idle chit-chat about farming, livestock prices, and all the new people moving up the mountain from the hot desert below.

Fredrick and Helga finally stood to go. "Thank you for the lovely cake, Dolly," Helga said, "and the first time you have free time, come see me and I'll take you on a walk to see the plants and herbs I use that grow up on this wonderful mountain of ours."

Fredrick grinned at Trace. "It sounds like my witch is trying to turn your girl into one as well."

Helga slapped her husband's back. "Watch your mouth, old man or you're liable to end up a hog rooting in the pig pen with all the others and I will have to be the one making the sausages."

They all laughed at the old woman's jest. "When you get back from your trip down to Conch," Fredrick said, "we'll put our heads together with my Lars and start building on to this place to give you, Dolly, and the little ones to come, some more room and a space for you to work."

Trace watched Dolly's face twist up in confusion. He hadn't spoken to her about his plans to add on to the cabin or travel back to Concho and empty the house.

"You're leaving?" Dolly ventured in a soft voice after Fredrick and Helga had departed.

Trace walked over and took Dolly into his arms. "I need to close up the house and pack up my tools," he told her. I'm moving up here for good to be with you." Trace pulled away. "Do you want me to tell Martin you're safe and out of Davis's hands?"

He watched Dolly shake her head ever so slightly. "Let the bastard think I'm still a slave in a San Francisco brothel where he sent me."

Trace kissed her, and she kissed him back, but she flinched away when his hand went to her bosom. "Damnit, Dolly," he swore. "Don't you know what you do to a man, prancing around, dressed in just your frillies like a little dancehall slut?" His voice came out of his mouth harsher than he intended.

He watched her bottom lip begin to tremble and tears brim in her blue eyes. "Take me back to Martin's then," she murmured, "and you can be done with this whore."

"That's not what I meant, Dolly." Trace sucked in his breath before he said something else hurtful. "I'm gonna buy a wagon down there in town and clean out the house and shop," he told her, "and when I get back after we've both had time to think on it, we'll talk about our future together."

He left the cabin without giving Dolly time to speak. What did she expect from him? He was a man and had the needs of a man—

more needs than just nice meals, pies, and cakes. Couldn't she understand that?

Trace saddled his horse, strapped his bedroll behind the saddle, filled two canteens, and stuffed a clean shirt into his saddle bag. He couldn't chance somebody recognizing Bess, so he left the gray mare with her saddle in the stable and made Davis's buggy horse ready to travel. It could pull the buckboard he intended to buy to haul the few contents of his house he wanted to bring and his tools up the mountain.

Before leaving, Trace went into the cabin and dropped a few coins onto the table in case Dolly had need to go into Vernon before he returned. She wasn't in the cabin. Perhaps she'd gone to use the outhouse.

He wanted to tell her good-bye but wasn't going to wait around for her. He opened the drawer of the little table and took out a piece of paper and a stubby pencil they used to make lists for the mercantile. He wrote: I'll be back in a week or two. Use the money however you see fit. Trace

Putting an apology on paper and then leaving didn't seem the right thing to do, so Trace left it as it was and returned to the horses.

14

Sleep that night didn't come easy to Dolly. She wept into her pillow, tossed and turned.

Dolly heard the howl of a wolf through the open window at the foot of her bed. She had no idea of the time. Trace didn't have a clock in the cabin. She thought it must be near sunup, though and threw off the blanket. She lit the lamp with a twig she stuck in the stove and then used the chamber pot.

The wolf howled again, but this time it sounded closer. She knew the chickens would attract predators, but Dolly hadn't expected anything quite so suddenly. Maybe the wolf had been attracted by the scent of the horses before she ever put the chickens out. She'd planned on releasing the birds into the coop, but perhaps she should wait for Trace to return.

Thinking about the man brought tears to her eyes again. Dolly took a cleansing breath and dashed them away. She refused to waste more time weeping. She wasn't certain what she would do next, but it certainly wouldn't be crying over a man who wanted a whore in his bed and not a true wife the way Lucy had been to him.

Keeping herself busy was the answer and Dolly began by making a pot of coffee. Her bucket was almost empty She'd need to make a few trips to the creek to fill the water barrel outside. That would account for a good hour or two of traipsing back and forth and Dolly welcomed it.

As her coffee boiled, Dolly mixed up a batch of bread. The scent of fresh bread baking filled the cabin with a homey aroma and always lifted her spirits.

The sun crested over the eastern horizon and Dolly stepped out onto the porch with a cup of coffee in her hand. One of the young roosters crowed roughly as young ones do and Dolly smiled. She lowered herself into the porch chair and pulled a shawl she'd found at the bottom of the wardrobe about her shoulders.

August would be upon them soon and with it the beginnings of cooler temperatures on the mountain. She needed to take the sickle and cut some grasses to dry for the cellar. The cabbages would be ready to cut soon and the potatoes ready to dig. She needed to get the bins ready to store them in.

The last time she'd ventured to the creek, she saw fat plums hanging in the thicket, not quite red yet. Dolly made note to check them today when she went for water. Soon after the plums ripened, Trace had told her the blackberries and raspberries growing along the creek would be ripe. Maybe it was time she went to the cellar and brought Lucy's mason jars up to wash and make ready. She would need more sugar for jams. Dolly made a mental note to add it to her list for the mercantile.

A thought suddenly came to Dolly as she sat enjoying the peace of the quiet mountain morning. This was the first time she'd been truly alone in her life. She stared up to see the branches of the tall pines swaying in the soft breeze. A few ominous gray clouds gathered in the sky to the south and the air felt heavy. Perhaps there would be rain today. The garden and the rain barrels could certainly use it.

Late summer saw storms pull up from the south, but as of yet they hadn't seen more than a few light showers. Trace had told her it happened like that some years and when the rains did come, they would be ferocious with high winds and thunder that shook the rafters. Dolly loved the rain. They got so little of it down in Concho that it was something to be celebrated when they did.

As Dolly slid the raw white loaves that had risen in the warm kitchen into the oven, she heard the first sound of thunder. She wrapped the shawl back around her shoulders and went out to feed the chickens and horses. It surprised her to see only Bess in the stable, but suspected Trace had taken Davis's horse with him for some reason. She gave Bess a quick currying and filled her trough with feed.

"It sounds like we're in for some weather, Bessie," Dolly said and patted the mare's neck. "I hope you're not spooked too badly by the thunder."

The first fat drops fell after Dolly had fed and watered the young chickens. It was a deluge by the time she reached the porch. "I sure hope Trace has a rain slicker with him or a place to hole up during this," Dolly mumbled to herself as she sat on the watching the rain fall through the thick green boughs of the pines. She sat enjoying the falling rain until she caught the scent of her bread and rushed inside to find it very brown and close to burning.

"Damn it," she hissed as she burned her fingers in a rush to get the loaves out of the oven. She'd only burned her bread once and Martin had delivered a beating Dolly had never forgotten.

"Who's gonna bake your bread now, I wonder," Dolly mumbled to herself as she put the crusty, brown loaves on the rack to cool.

She rubbed at the spot on her side where Martin had kicked her all those years ago, leaving a horrible purple bruise and a cracked rib that made it difficult to move or even breathe for several days. How had she allowed that to happen to her? Was there something she could have done?

Her brother had learned that behavior toward a woman from Daddy. Her father had beaten their mother and yelled terrible things at her. Naturally, Martin had transferred that to his younger sister when he'd been forced to take on her care.

"Maybe I should blame Daddy and not you, Martin, but Daddy was a hardworking man who put his money in the bank. And what did you do with it?" Dolly shook her head and threw her hands up in frustration. "It's too late for me to chew on it now, isn't it, Martin?"

The rain fell hard against the cedar roof of the cabin and Dolly could hear the wind howling. She wasn't certain which howling bothered her more—that of the wind now or the wolf the night before.

Dolly glanced up to see the bolts of fabric stacked neatly atop the tall wardrobe and smiled. This was just the sort of weather for cutting and sewing. She wouldn't need to carry water from the creek to fill the barrels and she wouldn't need to water the plants in the garden. All she needed to do today was cut fabric for the new things she'd need when she decided where she wanted to go and what she wanted to do once she got there.

Dolly pulled down the bolt of soft white cotton, rolled it out on the table and used a lead pencil to draw the pattern pieces for a night dress, dressing gown, camisole, petticoat, and bloomers. She'd never had bloomers before and thought they would be a nice addition to her wardrobe. She threw the small scraps she had cut away into the stove and saved the larger ones to use for collars, cuffs, and quilt pieces later. Dolly had learned to be frugal with her fabrics over the years.

She would make the night dress and dressing gown first. Dolly didn't intend to distress Trace ever again by walking around the place dressed like a dancehall slut. Those harsh words still brought tears to her eyes.

The sewing and the rain took her mind off everything that had happened over the last month and a half—the good and the bad. By the time true darkness fell, Dolly had completed the night dress and put it on. The fresh, soft cotton fabric felt good on her skin and she thought the next time she ventured to Vernon she would ask Mrs. Sanders about some flannel. A flannel nightdress and dressing gown would be good for the winter months on the mountain.

The Irishman stood over the wrecked buggy in the wet, sandy desert. Pauly wandered around somewhere between the buggy and the wagon they'd left on the narrow trail from Holbrook.

"You sure that's his buggy?" Pauly asked, when he sauntered up to join him.

"Yah, it be his," the Irishman said, with a sigh. "I recognize that little tear in the leather." He pointed to a one inch gap in the black leather upholstery in the middle of the buggy's seat. "I thought he'd have a damned cow when it happened."

"He did love his buggy," Pauly said with a nervous grin.

"Don't be speakin' of the man in the past tense." He took off his bowler and swatted Pauly with it. "We've found no body."

"I found two graves over yonder," Pauly told him, nodding back toward the trail, "and they look to be recent." He pulled at his sweaty shirt. "Could be those of Davis and the girl."

"Show me," the Irishman said, and they walked across the muddy terrain to two mounds of earth with rocks covering them against animals.

"Hey, boss," a female voice called from the wagon and he looked up to see a bare arm motioning to him from the barred window of the cat wagon. "Come here, boss."

He walked to the wagon with Pauly following close behind.

"Maybe she wants a poke," Pauly giggled.

The Irishman rolled his eyes. Did that fool think of nothing but his damned cock? He saw it was Millie, the oldest of the women on the wagon since he'd delivered Gert to Clegg in Colorado. "What ya yammerin' on about now, darlin'?"

"I saw that river or creek back there a ways," Millie said, rocking her mousey-brown head over her shoulder. "Me and the girls could use a bath, boss. It's been damned hot in here and Trixie's had her monthly runnin' down her legs all week. It's a right smelly mess in here."

The Irishman could smell the rank odor of over-ripe women and over-used chamber pot wafting from the wagon. He glanced around at the empty desert for miles around and saw no signs of life up or down the trail. He supposed it would be safe to let the women out to have a bit of a wash and clean up the wagon a bit. Clean cunny sold better than scummy.

The Irishman turned to Pauly. "Take the wagon and park it by the water," he said, nodding to the fast-moving waters of the creek. "The girls need a bath, the blankets need washin', and the piss-pots need a good scrubbin'."

Pauly grinned and squeezed his crotch. "I got somethin' here to scrub out their cunnies with."

"Find a nice flat spot by the water and build a fire," the Irishman said, shaking his head. "We'll camp here for a day or two before takin' the darlin's up to that gamblin' town on the mountain." He smiled. "There's always good money to be had up there."

Pauly climbed up onto the wagon. "I think I'll take the rifle and try to find us a rabbit or two for our supper. The whores may be able to survive on cock juice, but I need me some meat in my belly."

"That's the first productive idea you've offered all day, boyo. Take the wagon down and get the cunnies in the water first, though."

"Will do, boss." Pauly urged the horse into motion an turned the wagon around.

The Irishman watched the man park in a level sandy spot beside the creek. Pauly got down from the wagon and used his key to unlock the door at the rear. He barked orders as the emaciated, naked women climbed out of the wagon, dragging the chain that attached to a shackle on each woman's left ankle with them. The woman picked up rocks and built a fire ring, then went off to gather up pieces of dead cedar wood for a fire. One woman dragged the dirty, thread-bare blankets from the wagon and piled them and the chamber pot beside the water. Each woman would wash her blanket and throw it over a bush to dry.

Pauly strolled along the chained women putting his hands on their bosoms and between their legs. Before he allowed any of them into the water, he opened his trousers and made each woman get on her knees and play with his cock with her tongue.

The Irishman shook his head. Pauly was insatiable. He'd been known to go from woman to woman all night long. The wagon master, as the Irishman liked to think of himself, didn't know how the man did it.

Once all the women were in the water, Pauly took the rifle and wandered off into the cedars.

"You whores get yourselves all washed up now," the Irishman called out to the laughing women in the water. "I've a notion to poke some clean cunny tonight."

He smiled when he heard the crack of a rifle firing and then another. The Irishman hoped Pauly had been successful and they'd have fresh meat tonight. It had been too long, living on dry rations and salty jerky.

Pauly returned a half hour later with the skinned and gutted carcass of a young antelope over his shoulder. The eyes of the women went wide. This was more meat than the men could eat alone, and they knew they'd be allowed a share.

"Collect up more rocks for another pit," Pauly ordered the whores, "and wood too. We'll need two or three spits to cook all this 'lope' tonight."

Within a few minutes, the women had another ring of stones filled with wood and fitted with Y-shaped cedar branches for the meat Pauly stripped from the bone and portioned out. He held up a bloody leg bone and grinned at his boss. "I think I'm gonna poke the little Mex with this tonight and then watch her gnaw the meat off it."

"You'd best watch that one, Pauly," the Irishman said with a chuckle. "She's liable to gnaw the meat off your cock some night."

Pauly smiled through his bushy beard. "I don't mind a nip or two from time to time. It spices things up a might when they give me reason to slap 'em around some."

The women ate like greedy pigs, their faces and hands dripping with meat juice from the charred flesh they ate. Though warned by the older women to pace themselves and chew the meat completely, some ate so much of the meat so fast they threw it up almost immediately after swallowing.

Pauly sat beside his boss with meat juice glistening in his dark beard. "Which one you taking tonight, boss? I'd like the little Mex if you don't want her or we could pretend she's the redhead and both have a go at 'er."

The Irishman's cock stiffened at mention of the pretty redhead. He'd longed to watch her big bosoms bounce up and down as she rode his cock, but if she was moldering in one of those graves, that would never come to pass. "I think I'll take Millie tonight," he said, watching the older redheaded whore checking the dryness of the blankets.

Pauly snorted. "That dried up ol' cunny should have been left at Crane's with Greta." He tipped up a bottle of whiskey and gulped down the amber liquid. "What you think they done to her?"

The Irishman shrugged. "It's hard to say. I watched one fella beat and strangle a gal and another gut one like a fish and then fuck the hole in her belly all the time ravin', "How do you like that, Mother? How do you like that?"

Pauly shook his head. "That's disgustin'."

"You shoulda seen the time a fella spread this gal's legs and used a whiskey bottle to poke her. He shoved the damned thing in so far he could hardly keep hold of it, especially once it was slicked up with her blood." The Irishman shook his head. "And ya shoulda heard the awful screams and beggin' comin' from the pitiful old cow. It was almost heartbreakin'.

"She died?"

"Course, she died, you idgit," the Irishman snapped. "That's what they pay Crane to do. They pay him to kill a dirty, worthless whore once she's been all used up."

"How much do those fellas pay to kill a whore?" Pauly asked. "I've killed 'em just for the pleasure of it," he smirked, "and didn't pay nothin'."

"I heard Davis say a thousand once and them fellas that watch pay a hundred each." The Irishman shook his head, imagining that kind of money. "Sometimes he has a hundred or more in the room to watch. I guess some of them fellas like to kill in different ways every time and it draws a big crowd."

Pauly's eyes went wide. "You paid a hundred dollars to watch an old whore get poked to death with a bottle?"

"Oh, hell no. Davis and me were deliverin' a gal and we were invited by Crane to watch as that was the creative fella."

Pauly's gaze drifted to the pretty, young Mexican girl and he smiled. "I think I'll use my bottle here," he lifted the empty whiskey bottle in his hand, "and stretch out her cunny a little more."

"Just don't kill her," the Irishman warned.

"No, I prefer my women alive, but I don't mind none hearin' 'em scream and beg a little."

The Irishman's mind drifted back to the redhead and how good his cock had felt in her mouth while he watched tears of shame roll down her pretty cheeks. He stood and beckoned to Millie. "Get your cunnies chained back up and, in the wagon, Mil and then come back over here. My cock needs a little attention from your tongue."

"Sure thing, Paddy," she said with a forced grin before turning back to the women, "Collect your bedding, girls. It's time to get back in the wagon."

15

Trace crept back into town in the dead of night.
He'd been caught in the storm that first day and sheltered beneath some cottonwood trees until the worst had passed. He'd traveled in wet clothes until they dried on his back and then got rained on again two more times before getting to the base of the mountain.

He worried about Dolly, but suspected she'd keep herself busy inside until the storm passed. He hoped the wind hadn't done any damage. The cabin had needed new shingles for a while.

The house in Concho had been empty for some time now and smelled a little musty like it always had after his extended stays away on the mountain. Trace lit a lamp and stared around the parlor at all the things Lucy had purchased over the years. What would he take and what would he leave behind? Should he take Lucy's things to start a life with another woman?

Trace picked up the framed tin-type of his late wife and tears welled in his eyes. He couldn't help but feel unfaithful to Lucy for wanting to be with the young, pretty redhead so much.

"I know you liked her, Lucy, and thought we should do something for her when we heard Martin treating her the way he did." He wiped his eyes. "Well, I'm doin' it now."

Trace began to gather things up around the parlor. If he didn't think they would be practical or useful at the cabin, he left them. Lacey doilies were pretty, but he didn't think them very practical. In the end, he used the doilies to wrap Lucy's cut glass dishes in and put them in a crate to take.

As he emptied the kitchen shelves, someone pounded on the front door. Trace answered it with his heart pounding in his chest. It was Deputy Andy Green.

"Oh, hey, Trace. I didn't know you were back." The man Trace's age, who attended the same church as him, smiled. "Thought I'd best check on it when I saw the light."

"I just got back from doin' some huntin'," Trace told him. "As a matter of fact, I've got a nice young Elk on my horse out back and it's really more than I need. I'm sure you and Kate could use the meat with all those youngins of your's," Trace smiled, "if you want it."

The deputy smiled. "You're damned right I want it. Since the sheriff went missin' I haven't had time to hunt or even slaughter a hog."

"What happened to the sheriff?" Trace asked in an off-handed manner as he and Andy walked around the house to find two young elk draped over Davis's buggy horse.

"Wow," the deputy whistled, "you got two nice ones here."

"I've been out huntin' for a while and came across a small heard a few miles out of town," Trace said with a sigh. "I thought I'd see if Miss Mabel might want some fresh meat for her eatery. My smokehouse is full."

Andy studied the two carcasses with longing. "My damned smokehouse is almost empty. Ain't been able to do much for weeks now and Kate's about ready to skin my hide."

"Take 'em both, then, Andy." Trace began to untie the ropes holding the elk in place.

"I can't do that, Trace. I ain't got no money to pay ya for 'em like Miss Mabel."

Trace smiled at the man. "Take 'em, Andy. I don't need 'em and it's the Christian thing to do." He patted the deputy's shoulder. "Tell Kate to make you a nice steak supper on me."

"She's likely to come give you a big kiss." Andy hefted one of the carcasses off Trace's horse and onto his. "She does nothing but cuss Lucas for takin' off and leavin' me here in his stead to manage everything without pay."

"What do you mean without pay?" Trace asked as he untied the other elk and carried it to Andy's horse.

"The manager at the bank said Lucas told him nobody except him was to have access to the Law Fund Account and he won't release enough for my or Willy's pay."

"Have you spoken to Mayor Brody about it? He, if anybody, could override the sheriff's orders and get you your pay."

"Brody's a damned cunny and scared to death of Lucas," Andy swore, "He's afraid Lucas will come back and have a cow if he dips into the account for any reason."

"That's just silly," Trace said. "He's the Mayor of this town and the money in that account belongs to the town—not sheriff Lucas."

"Lucas doesn't want anyone to know how much is actually in that damned account," Andy snorted. "I know he's gettin' a percentage from the saloon for the girls workin' there and the Ross brothers are payin' him to look the other way when they acquire cattle from other herds and rebrand 'em with their fancy back to back Rs."

Trace's eyes went wide. "I had no idea." Trace was feeling less and less guilty for putting the man in the ground. "Where the hell has he gotten off to anyway?"

Andy shrugged his shoulders. "Hell if I know. He rode out of town with that fella from San Francisco when he took Dolly Stroud away, and we ain't heard from him since."

"Maybe he went to California with the man."

"And with Dolly," Andy said with a chuckle. "Did you see that show her and that fella put on in the window?" Andy shook his head. "Sure wish I'd known she was that kinda girl."

Trace felt his face going red. "You're a married man with children, Andy."

"Nothin' says a man can't consort with a whore every now and again," Andy said with a grin. "Especially when his wife is heavy with child or just after when her cunny is all stretched out and bloody. Least ways that's what all the fellas down at the saloon say."

"Just what else are all the fellas down at the saloon sayin'?"

Andy smiled and leaned his head in close. "I heard tell ol' Martin's been sharin' his bed with his little redheaded sister all these years and was the one who taught her all those whore tricks she showed off in that window."

Trace clinched his fists in rage. "Is that so?"

"Dolly never popped over across the street to share her favors with you, Trace?"

Trace frowned down at the deputy. "No, and I don't think the fellas down at the saloon know what they're talkin' about. Dolly's a good, church-goin' girl."

"I think she had everyone fooled. I know she'll never be allowed to step foot in the church again after that little show she put on here and out with that whore wagon."

"What are you talking about?"

"I heard tell that after she put on her show here, that fella took Dolly out to the edge of town where his whore wagon was parked and every fella who watched here took turns with her out there." Andy paused and grinned. "Sometimes two or three at a time. I'd have surely loved to have seen a thing like that."

"I'm sure," Trace said, barely containing his rage. "Well, you'd better get that elk gutted before it spoils the meat and be sure to give Kate my best."

Trace hoped saying the man's wife's name would send him on his way.

"You're right, Trace," Andy said and patted the rump of one of the elk, "and thanks again for the meat. Kate and the kids will really appreciate it."

"No worries," Trace mumbled as the deputy rode away.

He returned to the small house he'd shared with Lucy and

continued to pack. Dolly could never return to Concho. She was ruined here. Trace finished with the kitchen and went into the bedroom. Could he take the bed he'd shared with Lucy up the mountain to share with another woman? He sat and ran a hand over the quilt Lucy had stitched the year she died. No, this would remain here.

Trace glanced out the window and saw a light come up in Martin's house. He must be getting home from one of his late night excursions to the saloon. How could he show his face in public when everyone thought what they thought about him?

Trace knew it wasn't true. Dolly still had her maiden head and while she'd been used by Davis, the sheriff, and that Irishman, it hadn't been something Dolly wanted or had sought out.

Trace came close to marching across the street and telling Martin Stroud exactly what he thought about him, but he didn't. Instead, Trace kicked off his boots and reclined on the comfortable bed he'd shared with Lucy. He hadn't thought he'd ever want another woman after Lucy, but Dolly's face and that mass of red hair kept pushing into his thoughts.

He'd given up on the idea of having children as well, but Dolly was still young. She might be able to give him a son. She wasn't little like Lucy had been. Maybe Dolly's body could endure birthing a child of his.

Trace fell into a fitful sleep and woke to the sound of Dolly's rooster crowing across the street. He was surprised to find the bird still alive with Martin left to tend him. He glanced out the window into the Stroud's back yard to see Dolly's neat garden overgrown with weeds and the chickens roaming outside their coop. He supposed Martin found it easier to let them feed in the garden.

Packing up his tools in the shop took him longer than expected, but by noon, Trace left the house with Davis's horse in tow and went to buy a wagon from one of the local farmers who'd had one for sale the last time Trace had visited. First, he went to the bank and withdrew all his funds.

"Is there a problem, Mr. Anderson?" the bank manager Herman Evans asked after the teller had gone in to tell him one of their oldest customers was withdrawing his considerable funds and closing his account.

Trace considered his words. "I've decided to return home to Texas, Herm. I think it's time."

The bank manager's eyes went wide. "What are you going to do with the house? Have you sold it?"

"Not yet." Trace hadn't considered selling the house. He didn't know how he'd manage it now.

"We can handle that for you here, Mr. Anderson. We've recently added an Estate Division, dealing with the sales and transfers of property."

"The deed is in my safe deposit box along with an extra key," Trace said.

"That's very good," the banker said. "I'll just need you to come in my office and sign a power of attorney, giving me the authority to act on your behalf in the matter of the sale, and your safe deposit box key."

Trace signed everything the banker asked him to sign and was certain he'd never see a dime from the sale of the house. He'd never trusted the slimy banker, but Trace was ready to walk away from his past in Concho and his past with Lucy. That included the house. It was time to walk away and begin a new life.

The farmer and Trace settled on a price for the wagon and he hitched up the horse. He took the wagon home and began to load it up. As he did, Martin Stroud came sauntering over dressed in a fancy black suit and shiny new boots. On his head he wore a black bowler hat with a cock's feather stuck in one side over his ear. Trace's stomach churned, and he clenched his fists in rage.

"Where ya headed, Anderson? Looks like you're getting out of Concho for good." Martin released a long sigh. "Sure wish I was going."

"What's keepin' ya now that Dolly's gone?" Trace asked, wondering what the cocky little dandy's answer would be.

"I expect her back any day now," Martin said with an uneasy look on his face.

"The trip to San Francisco I heard tell about was only temporary then?"

Martin's eyes went wide. "Who said she went to San Francisco?"

Was he kidding? "Martin, every man down at the saloon knows she went off to San Francisco with that dude in his buggy to be a whore and that you sold her to him after you'd trained her up to be just that." Trace pointed his finger at Dolly's gaping brother. "A dirty whore." He tried his best to make the comment feel like he was accusing him of doing that to his innocent sister.

"I did no such thing." Martin denied in an indignant tone.

"I was just at the bank, Martin," Trace sneered. "Herman told me that fella bought your mortgage and others have told me he bought up your gambling debts." Trace shook his head in disgust and spat into the street. "What sorta man sells his sister to a whoremaster to cover his own ass?"

As Trace turned to return to his loading, Martin spoke again. "Dolly went of her own accord, Anderson. She wanted to go with Davis and whore for him. I didn't force the lazy little cunny to do anything."

Trace balled up his fists, trembling with rage. "Are you sayin' your little sister wanted to be a whore?"

"No, of course not," Martin spat. "She wanted to go with him because she didn't want Lucas to throw me in jail or that man to take my house." Martin motioned toward the house in sore need of a paint job. "That lazy little bitch owed me, and she knew it. She —"

Martin didn't get the chance to finish his rant. Trace drew back his balled fist and landed a punch to the dandy's mouth that sent the bowler hat flying into the muddy street and the worthless man with it.

Trace stepped over to stare down at the man trying to get back on his feet in the slipper mire. "Dolly didn't owe you a damned thing, Martin. After ten years of cookin' your meals, cleanin' your house, and takin' your foul-mouthed abuse, I'd say the girl had paid any debt she might have owed an older brother who was bound, as her only family left, to look after her."

Trace used his boot to push the floundering man back into the mud. "Dolly deserved a hell of a lot better than you, Martin, and you didn't deserve a sister like her." Trace spat into the street again, turned and stormed back into his house.

With a feeling of satisfaction, Trace finished loading the wagon with pieces of furniture he thought Dolly might like to have or find useful. He wasn't certain where they'd put them in the small cabin, but perhaps when he and Fredrick had added the rooms they'd discussed, Dolly would have room aplenty for settees, side tables, vanities, and china hutches.

Trace remembered how Lucy had smiled and fussed over every new household item and he missed seeing that sort of joy on a woman's face. He wondered what Dolly would do when she saw what he'd brought.

As Trace and his wagon left Concho, Herman Evans drew up in a buggy to the Anderson property and posted a For Sale sign on the fence.

16

The storming on the mountain lasted three days. When it finally stopped raining, Dolly had new night things in the wardrobe, a set of new underthings on her body, and a new riding skirt and blouse nearly finished.

She'd feared for the garden, but upon inspection, she saw no standing water between the rows and no plants matted down in the mud from the pounding rains. Everything stood green and healthy. With a little sunshine, Dolly expected blooms on the potatoes soon and the first batches of sweet peas and green beans. She'd scrubbed and boiled the canning jars and lids. Everything was in readiness for the harvests.

A week after Trace had gone, Dolly got her monthly and was glad she'd stitched up a few clouts from scrap fabric and had them ready. She didn't want to stain her new things and wondered if Mrs. Sanders stocked the garter she needed to hold the pads in place. Dolly had done her best to improvise one, but it was awkward and time consuming. She needed a garter and added that to her list for the mercantile in Vernon.

The rain had filled the water barrels, but Dolly wanted to check on the plums. She took her basket and strolled toward the thicket near the creek. The storms had caused the water to rise considerably and it rushed over the rocks at a tremendous speed.

The wind had sent ripe, red plums to the ground and Dolly picked up enough to nearly fill her basket. She tasted one and the skin was tart with sweet juicy flesh inside. The fall had bruised some of the fruit, but Dolly intended to make them into plum butter anyhow. She finished filling the basket with low-hanging fruit and returned to the cabin proud of her bounty.

She'd turned the young chickens out into the coop and threw them a few of the most bruised plums to enjoy. She fed Bess and filled her trough with water. The few weeds that had sprung up in the garden would have to wait until the ground firmed up some. Dolly took her basket into the kitchen, washed the plums and put them into a pot of water to boil and loosen the skins.

Lucy's hand-written cookbook held the recipe for the butter Trace told Dolly he loved. She went through the pages until she found it and then gathered the ingredients together. Dolly had known Lucy well and admired the woman. It had broken her heart when she'd heard Lucy had died giving birth to the child she'd wanted to give Trace so very badly.

Dolly sat with tears brimming in her eyes, remembering how happy Lucy had been when she'd realized it had been three months since she'd bled last and knew she finally carried Trace's child after waiting and praying for so long.

She and Lucy had sat together for hours in Lucy's parlor, sewing baby clothes and quilts that would never be used. Dolly wondered what had become of them. She knew Trace had taken Lucy's clothes to the church to be distributed to the poor. Perhaps he'd done the same with the baby's things.

Over the next two hours, Dolly followed the directions written in Lucy's beautiful, flowing script to produce six pint jars of the thick, sweet plum butter. It took most of the sugar left in the tin as well as the cinnamon and Dolly added those to her list of things to get at the mercantile.

Once she'd tightened the lids on the six jars and boiled them in the canning pot to seal, Dolly took her sewing to the chair on the porch to add the buttons onto the blouse and hem the two sections of the divided riding skirt. Tomorrow, she'd try the new skirt out with a ride into Vernon for the supplies she needed. Dolly reckoned there were enough ripe plums on the trees for another basket and six more jars.

The following morning, after some toasted bread smeared with some of the plum butter, Dolly fed the chickens and Bess. She patted the gray mare's neck. "How about a ride today, girl?"

Dolly went inside and put on the skirt she'd made from heavyweight black poplin. She couldn't wear a petticoat with it and had put on the pair of bloomers she'd just made instead. The garments felt odd to Dolly after a lifetime in petticoats and skirts, but they were certainly more practical for riding.

She added the yoked blouse she'd made from blue and red plaid cotton with a few lines of black in it to accent the skirt. Dolly had trimmed the yoke with some of the narrow lace to add a feminine touch to the otherwise manly outfit. Dolly put on her boots and studied herself in the mirror. She turned a few times and concluded she didn't look manly in the least. With some of the remaining black poplin she'd make a jacket for the cooler months.

Dolly opened the little drawer in the table between the chairs in the parlor and took out Trace's note and the silver coins he'd left her. She wondered where he was and when or if he'd be back. She slipped two of the heavy silver coins into one of the deep pockets she'd added to the skirt along with her folded list. Dolly went to the stable and saddled Bess for the long trip into Vernon.

"Are you ready for that ride, girl?" Dolly asked in a cheerful tone. She'd been cooped up too long and looked forward to a day out in the fresh air and sunshine. She also longed to hear the voice of another human being.

Dolly lifted her leg to put her foot in the stirrup, hefted herself up, and swung her other leg over the saddle. She had to admit the riding skirt was quite comfortable and much more practical than riding in a regular skirt. Her ankles and bare shins weren't exposed in an unseemly fashion and the insides of her thighs wouldn't be worn raw from riding astride like a man.

The day was beautiful with sunny skies and a slight breeze coming up from the south. Dolly hoped that didn't mean more rain, but she didn't see any clouds building in that direction and sighed with relief.

When she came upon the Snydergaard farm, Dolly saw Fredrick and Helga both out in the garden. She reined Bess into the lane and rode up toward the smiling couple.

"Gooten morn, Mrs. Anderson," Fredrick greeted with a broad smile on his weathered face. "What are you doing out on this fine day?"

"Riding into Vernon for some supplies," Dolly replied.

Helga walked over with a hoe in her gnarled hand. "Is that man of your's not returned yet?"

Dolly's face lost its smile at the thought of Trace's absence. "Not yet, but I'm hoping it will be soon."

Fredrick waved a hand in a dismissive fashion. "If he left before the rains, it probably slowed him and if it's been raining down there he's probably trapped in his house. He'll be back soon." He reached up and patted Dolly's hand. "How could he stay long away from a pretty woman like you?"

Dolly blushed as she reached into her pocket and took out a pint jar and handed it to Helga. "I made some plum butter yesterday."

The old woman took the jar with a smile on her face. "Thank you, child. When our apples are ripe in another few months we will make apple butter together. Yes?"

So this was where the apples in the cellar had come from. "Indeed we will, Helga. I look forward to it." Dolly turned back to Fredrick. "I stopped because I need more milk."

"I'll bring more tomorrow," he said, "and pick up the empty can."

"I washed out the empty one for you," Dolly told him as she reached into her pocket for a coin. "How much do I owe you?"

"Put your money away, child," Helga said, "you've more than paid for a can of milk with this." She held up the jar in her hand.

Fredrick added, "Trace has already paid me for several cans of milk, Dolly."

"Oh, I didn't know."

"Lucy and I used to trade things like this," Helga told her. "She had her plums, blackberries, and raspberries, and I have my apples, peaches, and cherries."

Dolly smiled. "That's good to know. Those plum trees are loaded. I'll bring you a basket in a day or two."

"And I'll bring you milk tomorrow."

Dolly shook her head. "Wait until the day after and I'll have plums for you to bring back to Helga."

Fredrick smiled and put his arm around Helga. "I can taste the plum pudding already."

"Ha," Helga snorted, "maybe if you cook it. I have cheeses to make."

Dolly turned Bess and left the old couple to their good-natured bickering. She enjoyed the breeze in her hair as she rode and the scent of pine in the air. The aroma of freshly-milled wood and the sound of trees being cut filled the air as she rode past a section of forest being harvested.'

Dolly's breath caught in her throat when she spotted a very familiar wagon parked in a clearing not far from the lumber operation. She heard the voices of women and saw a group of burly lumbermen lounging around a firepit. She didn't see the Irishman or the other man she'd seen with him and the wagon, but Dolly was certain he must be somewhere about. She kicked Bess into a trot and hoped she hadn't been noticed as she passed.

Her backside burned by the time she got off Bess at Sanders' Mercantile in Vernon. As she'd done before, Mrs. Sanders greeted her with a cup of cool, sweet water.

"You're Trace Anderson's wife, aren't you?" the middle-aged woman asked as she glanced out the window. "Is he with you?"

"No, I came in alone. Trace had to go back down to Concho to check on the house there and his business."

"Mrs. Sanders nodded. "He does fine work," she said. "I love having his things in the store. They sell out almost as quick as I set them out on the shelves." She smiled. "Trace is a good trading partner."

Dolly smiled. Perhaps Trace will have a market up here for his goods after all.

"He should really talk to some of these lumbermen," Mrs. Sanders continued. "They're always after harnesses and such for their tree climbing."

"I'll be sure to tell him when he gets back." Dolly reached into her pocket for her list. "These are the things I need." She handed the list to Mrs. Sanders and noticed a display of jams and jellies stacked on the counter. Pieces of pinked fabric had been draped over the top of the jars sealed with wax rather than metal lids. The fabric was held in place with pieces of ribbon in coordinating colors tied in bows. Dolly thought it looked charming.

"Do you trade for things like this as well?" Dolly asked.

"I did," Mrs. Sanders said with a sigh, but old Mrs. Demming just passed away. Those are the last of the jars I got from her."

Dolly nodded with an idea forming in her head. Why should Trace be the only good trading partner? "I'm going to just look around while you gather my order, ma'am."

"Please go right ahead," the woman told Dolly. "I have a whole table back in the back filled with fabric fresh down from Denver. It's mostly heavier winter fabric like flannel and wool."

"Thank you, ma'am. I'll have a look."

Dolly rushed through the aisles, ignoring the sweet-smelling balls of soap and bright, cut-glass lamp shades. The sight of so much fabric took Dolly's breath away. She'd always loved to sew and had been making her own dresses since the age of ten when her mother first put a needle and thread into her hand. By the time her parents died, Dolly was making shirts and jackets for both her brother and father.

Puzzles were something Dolly had always enjoyed, and it hadn't taken her long to discover the fact that dress patterns were nothing more than puzzle pieces that when made in the right shape could be sewn together to create a dress or shirt. Dolly had studied the pictures of dresses in periodicals to figure out new patterns. She'd received many complements over the years from the women at church for the dresses and bonnets she'd made.

Dolly had a bolt of pristine white flannel in her hand when Mrs. Sanders appeared beside her. "Isn't that blouse made from the fabric you and Trace bought a few weeks ago? It's absolutely lovely." The woman fingered the fabric as she studied Dolly's seams.

Dolly felt her cheeks flush. "And I used the poplin to make this riding skirt too." She tugged at the skirt with both hands to show the woman how it was split up the center with a crotch like men's trousers.

"That's amazing," the woman gasped. "How ever did you think of it?"

"I saw it in a fashion periodical," Dolly admitted. "I don't ride side-saddle, so I thought this would be perfect."

"It would be perfect for climbing ladders in this store too," Mrs. Sanders said with a sigh as she studied Dolly and her clothes. "I fear I'm all thumbs when it comes to thimbles and needles. My dear mother used to tell me I'd better marry a rich man who could afford a seamstress for me." She smiled at Dolly.

"Would you consider making one of those for me? I'd pay you, of course." The woman grinned. "And a blouse like that too."

Dolly slipped her hands into the deep pockets. "Would you want pockets like this too?"

Mrs. Sanders' eyes went wide. "Lord, yes, girl. Those would be so handy to have around here. What would you charge me?"

Dolly was at a loss. She'd never thought about being paid for her work before. She still held the bolt of flannel in her hands. "How many yards are in these bolts?"

"Ten if I'm not mistaken." Mrs. Sanders replied. "Why?"

Dolly walked around the woman, studying her shape. "You look to be about my size, but we should use a cloth tape to be certain. It took six yards of fabric to make this—four for the skirt and two for the blouse." Dolly went to the other table and picked up a bolt of calico. "I could make a dress for me or you from this and have enough left over to make a shirt for Trace or your husband."

"You make men's clothes too?" Mrs. Sanders asked with an arched brow.

Dolly grinned and wrinkled her nose. "I don't care for making trousers, but I can. I made all my brother's clothes for a long time, but I prefer making dresses, blouses, and other women's things."

"Wait here for a minute," the woman said before scurrying away toward the front of the store.

Mrs. Sanders returned a few minutes later with a fashion periodical Dolly recognized. She opened it to a page and pointed to a color plate of a woman wearing a fancy dress made with a lot of lace and a flouncy bustled apron. "Can you make that?"

It would be a complicated pattern and take considerably more than six yards of fabric, but it was doable. Dolly smiled at the eager-faced woman. "I can make that, but it will take a good bit of extra fabric, lace, and ribbon."

"I've wanted a dress like this ever since I opened up to that page," she said, "but never thought to have one." She screwed her face up in a frown. "Vernon needs a good dressmaker, but it's not big enough to attract one like Prescott, Flagstaff, or even St. Johns." The woman took Dolly's hands. "I'll pay you anything you ask to make that dress for me, Mrs. Anderson."

17

After three days of hard travel up the mountain, Trace arrived back at the cabin to find it empty.

The first thing he did was go to the wardrobe and fling it open. Inside he found a woman's night dress and dressing gown on hangers and the dress Dolly had made. Then he saw her old underthings in a pile on the floor at the foot of the bed.

Trace sighed with relief to see she still inhabited the cabin and hadn't run off in a huff over him leaving her all alone. In the parlor he saw the drawer partially opened and suspected she'd gone to Vernon for supplies.

On the rack above the stove Trace found a pan of cornbread and two fresh loaves of bread. On the pie safe, he found six jars filled with plum butter and one partially filled jar. Trace smiled. It looked as though Dolly had kept herself busy in his absence.

He sliced off some of the bread and slathered on some of the plum butter. Trace smiled. It tasted just like Lucy's. When he'd finished, Trace went out to take the horses to the stable, water, feed them, and rub them down after the long ride up the mountain.

Trace shook his head upon seeing Dolly had already filled the trough with water and the bin with feed. How could Martin have ever called the girl lazy?

While he wanted to do nothing more than change his shirt, drop into his chair on the porch, and put his feet up, Trace went back to the stable and saddled his horse. Something nagged at him, telling him he needed to go meet Dolly on the trail. He needed to apologize to her and tell her how he felt.

Trace heaved his big, tired body into the saddle and headed toward Vernon. When he came upon Fredrick cutting weeds along the edge of his property and the trail he slowed his horse and stopped.

Fredrick set aside his cutting tool and walked to Trace with a smile on his wrinkled, suntanned face. "You in search of that wife of your's, boy?"

"Have you seen her?"

"She stopped by this morning on her way in to Vernon. She ordered some milk and brought me and the misses a jar of plum butter she made." Fredrick smiled up at Trace. "You've got yourself a fine woman there, Trace."

"I hope I still have her."

Fredrick arched a brow. "What do you mean by that?"

"We had harsh words before I left."

"Achh," Fedrick said with a wave of his work-worn hand, "If Helga had left me every time we exchanged harsh words, there'd never have been nine babies."

Trace chuckled. "Maybe she got them making up after the harsh words."

The old man chuckled. "In that case there'd have been a lot more than nine."

Both men laughed. Fredrick stopped suddenly and furrowed his brow. "I should have warned her this morning," the old man said with a sigh, "but I didn't think about it until Dolly had gone."

Something twisted in Trace's gut. "Warned Dolly about what, Fredrick?"

"A new logging operation has moved up onto the ridge," he said.

Trace was confused. "Why would you need to warn her about that? Those fellas tend to keep to their work back in the trees."

"That's the thing," the old man said, "They're not keeping to the trees."

"Why?" Trace asked with an uneasiness building in his gut.

"Because one of those whore wagons has parked up there just past where they're working and them fellas can smell cunny a mile off." Fredrick ran a hand over his sweaty, thinning hair. "I should have warned your woman there might be lumbermen with hard cocks roaming the road up ahead."

"Don't worry about my Dolly, Fredrick. She can take care of herself." Trace tried to sound confident, but he didn't know if he pulled it off. "The last time we were in Vernon, I watched her punch a man in the face and send him to the saloon floor for getting frisky with her after we'd had our lunch."

Fredrick grinned. "She sounds like my Helga when she was younger. She let no man take liberties but me."

With his nerves now on edge, Trace took his leave of the old farmer. "I'm gonna ride on ahead and meet her. I'll see you when you deliver the milk and we'll get started on the plans for those additions I want to build."

"We'll do that," the old man said, "and tell that girl of your's I already opened that jar of plum butter and it's as good as any your Lucy ever made."

"I'll do that," Trace said with a wave as he headed on up the trail. He knew he'd only tell her Fredric thought it was good. He knew enough about women to know it would rile one to be compared with another.

Trace kept his horse moving at a steady pace. He couldn't honestly say he was worried for Dolly in a confrontation with lumberman, but Fredrick's mention of a whore wagon brought back memories of that Irishman and his wagon.

Could it be the same wagon? Trace didn't think so. From his hiding place in the cedars, Trace had clearly heard Davis tell the man to make the rounds of the military forts in the north and then head to someplace in Colorado. Could they have made it to

Colorado and back here already? Maybe they were back searching for Davis — and Dolly.

His gut wrenched again. If they'd gone back to where Davis had left them, they might have come across the wrecked buggy and the two graves. Maybe they'll think the two are dead and were simply going on about their way when they stumbled upon the lumber operation and the Irishman saw a prime business opportunity.

Trace rode on for another hour before he heard the sounds of the lumber operation. He'd prayed there would be a sign of Dolly, but he hadn't seen her. If she'd left the cabin early, shopped in Vernon, and maybe had a lunch, Trace expected to run into her anytime. He saw laughing men walking along the trail and knew where they were headed and returning from. He prayed Dolly hadn't run afoul of that Irishman and was now chained naked in that wagon being used by these sweaty lumbermen.

He took a breath and urged his horse ahead. He was determined to find Dolly and bring her home.

18

By the time Dolly left Mrs. Sanders' mercantile she'd measured the woman in her apartment above the store and had orders for the fancy dress, two split skirts with blouses, and three shirts each for Mrs. Sanders' husband and son. The woman had given Dolly two of the men's old shirts to take apart for patterns.

"So what are you going to charge me for this, Mrs. Anderson?" the storekeeper had asked.

Dolly thought about it. "I'd reckon on a trade, ma'am. For every dress I make for you and one shirt for your men, I'd trade you one bolt of cloth."

Mrs. Sanders' mouth fell open. "You only want one bolt of cloth for all that work?"

"I see it as a fair trade," Dolly said. "You get finished garments and I receive the cloth to make the same for Trace and I." Dolly smiled. "I'll still have to purchase my notions from you or trade you for jam."

Mrs. Sanders' eyes went wide. "Of course you cook too. Trace is one lucky man to have you, girl." She smiled. "And you're a shrewd bargainer as well."

They chatted in the apartment over coffee and cookies. "Do you think you can have that dress done before the Summer Soiree in three weeks?"

"As long as you send along all the fabric and notions with me today, I'm sure I can."

The picture of the garment in the fashion periodical was obviously meant to be made of silk or satin for a high society party, but Dolly talked Mrs. Sanders into making it from a simpler cotton fabric trimmed with lots of lace, satin ribbon, and pearl buttons.

"Vernon isn't New York City, ma'am," Dolly had pointed out, "and you don't want the people who are your customers here to think you're putting on airs. This dress made from a simple calico can be worn to that dance and to church functions with only a change of the gloves and bonnet you wear."

Mrs. Sanders' mouth fell open as she pondered Dolly's words. "You're absolutely right, Mrs. Anderson. I never would have thought about how wearing a dress made from fancy fabric like satin would look to the other ladies in the community." She refilled Dolly's cup. "You really are a wonder, Mrs. Anderson. I'm sure that if you opened a shop in Vernon, you'd have more business than you could handle."

Dolly's face flushed again. "It's much too far for me to travel to open a shop in Vernon, Mrs. Sanders." She reached out and patted the woman's hand. "Why don't I sew for you and if you've a mind, you can refer customers to me from time to time."

"Please call me Vivian," Mrs. Sanders said as she stood for Dolly to take her measurement.

"And please call me Dolly."

Vivian whipped around with a flourish of her arms. "Oh, I can see the sign above your shop now, 'Dolly's Dressier, Custom Lady's Ware for the Practical Woman in Vernon'. What do you think, Madame Dolly?"

Dolly giggled. "Just give me that tape, Vivian."

Vivian Sanders measured smaller around the bosoms than Dolly, larger in the waist and hips, and two inches shorter. Dolly marked it down on the back of the list she'd brought from home and returned it to her pocket.

"That's all I'll need to draft the pattern," Dolly said. "I'd best be heading back if I want to make it before dark."

"Donald loaded your horse, Dolly, but you'd best take it slow. I don't want you to wash and iron that dress before it's even made."

"Don't worry, ma'am, I'll be very careful."

Bess was loaded down with bolts of fabric, bundles of notions, and sacks of sugar, salt, and flour. She'd needed eggs, but Mrs. Sanders hadn't any in stock. Dolly thought it just as well. She'd probably have broken them before she made it home anyhow.

"I'm sorry, Bess," Dolly told the horse after she'd mounted, "but I promise to give you an extra-long currying when we get home."

With the afternoon sun at her back, Dolly tried to keep Bess moving in the shade of the pines and poplars, growing along the trail. Dolly felt the bolts of fabric stacked behind her and smiled.

She could earn a living with her sewing. Vivian's words rattled around in her head. 'Dolly's Dressier' sounded so fancy. She could see a shop with a big window and fancy dresses on dress forms in that window. All the dresses would have matching bonnets.

Dolly glowed with pride. Somebody actually wanted to pay her to sew for them and trusted her to do a good job of it. She felt a flicker of doubt and fear for a minute. What if Vivian didn't like the dress? What if she messed it up somehow?

Dolly heard her brother's voice in her head again calling her lazy and stupid. She swept Martin's voice from her head. She wasn't lazy. She'd always worked every day from the time she rose in the morning until she retired at night and she still did.

He'd come home early one afternoon and caught her reading in the shade outside and demanded she get off her lazy behind and fix his supper. Her work had been done and it was well before suppertime, but her brother had beaten and chastised her none the less. It caused self-doubt to nag at Dolly. She'd make Vivian's dress right away and take care doing it, making certain every stitch was uniform and every button sewn down tightly.

Dolly told herself she was neither lazy nor slothful. She wasn't stupid either. Stupid people didn't make good trades like the one she'd made today. She went to Vernon with three dollars in her pocket and she was returning home with poor Bess loaded down and still two of the big silver dollars in her pocket. Martin had certainly never managed to do anything like that.

She couldn't help but worry about her hapless brother. Who was taking care of him now? He certainly couldn't take care of himself. Dolly knew Martin had never so much as fried an egg. Had he let the fire in the stove go out?

Dolly rode along and kept Bess at a slow pace. She had her mind filled with thoughts of her brother and didn't notice the man step out of the bushes along the side of the trail.

"Well now," the Irishman said as he grabbed Bess's halter, "if it ain't me cocksuckin' redhead."

His voice and the sudden stop jolted Dolly to attention and her heart skipped a beat as she stared at the man leering up at her.

"What happened to our Mr. Davis, darlin'? I can't fathom him lettin' you wander about alone through the countryside like this." The man studied the things loaded on Bess. "Sent ya on a shoppin' trip, has he? You must be takin' right good care of the man for that." He stepped closer and grabbed Dolly's calf. "Where the hell is he, girl?"

Dolly sat speechless for a moment. "He's dead and buried," she finally told the man with his fingers digging into her skin and began kicking at the Irishman who refused to release her calf.

"Stop that fussin' now," he said and yanked on Dolly's leg with a smile on his face. "If Davis is dead then that means the wagon and the sluts are mine now." He squeezed and yanked harder on Dolly's leg, trying to pull her from the saddle. "That means you're mine too."

"Get your filthy hands off me, you bastard," Dolly yelled as loudly as she could. "I don't belong to anybody." She managed a satisfying kick to the man's face.

That enraged the Irishman and he released the rein holding Bess to grab Dolly's leg. She clinched her legs to hold the horse tight, but the man was unseating her.

"Get down here and let Paddy relieve you of that virginity ol' Mr. Davis held in such high regard." He tugged hard to pull the young woman down from her perch. "You'll be comin' to me wagon to suck cock and get poked, so ya won't be needin' it anymore."

Dolly had wrapped the leather reins around her arms and bent over the saddle to hold on to Bess. "Leave me be," Dolly screamed with tears of rage sliding down her cheeks. How could this be happening to her again? How could this be happening when she'd just glimpsed an independent future for herself. She was going to be a seamstress not a whore in a dirty wagon.

Dolly tried to make Bess move, but the confused animal remained in one place. "Let's go, Bess," Dolly yelled, but the horse refused to move.

"Seems your animal thinks you should come with ol' Paddy here," the Irishman said with an angry chuckle as he tugged again on Dolly's leg. "If you don't come down from there, I'm gonna give ya the beatin' of your life, darlin'," the Irishman grinned up at her, "and then I'm gonna give ya to Pauly. That man enjoys dolin' out discipline to the whores and I don't think you'll be enjoyin' his methods."

Dolly had endured plenty of beatings in her life and she didn't want to endure anymore, but she certainly wasn't going to give herself over to this Irish bastard to become one of his whores. "Get the hell off me," she screamed and kicked again.

The kick loosened Dolly's grip on Bess with her legs and the Irishman's tug unhorsed her. She slid from the saddle, but her arms remained tangled in the reins. Dolly hung awkwardly from the horse with her hands above her head.

"Now that's more like it," the Irishman said as he twisted Dolly around to face him. He rubbed at the red spot on his face where Dolly had landed her kick. "I'm thinkin' I owe you a bit for this though."

He drew back his arm and punched Dolly in the stomach. The impact jolted Bess and she took a few steps, but the man grabbed the horse's halter and stopped her. "Just hold still girl," he said in the soothing tone used for skittish animals, but Dolly wasn't certain he'd spoken to Bess or her as he began to unbutton her blouse. "I wanna see what's under here again," he said with an absurd giggle, "before Pauly gets at 'em. That boy likes to bite, ya know, and more than one of me lasses is missin' a nipple." He giggled again, "or two."

The pain from the punch began to recede but the rage only built as the man opened her blouse and then her camisole to bare Dolly's bosoms and suck a nipple into his mouth while pinching the other and kneading her tender flesh.

"Get the hell off me, you bastard," Dolly screamed as loudly as she could into his ear before biting it until she tasted his coppery blood in her mouth.

The Irishman screamed and jerked away from Dolly as he slapped a hand to his bleeding ear. "You'll pay for that, bitch," he yelled and slapped Dolly hard.

She grinned and spit the piece of his ear she'd been holding between her teeth at his feet. "Watch what you try to put in my mouth or it's liable to go missing parts of it too."

"Fucking bitch," he screamed and began slapping Dolly as hard as he could, one cheek and then the other. "You'll pay, bitch. I'm takin' you to Pauly and you'll pay dearly." He stared from the blood on his hand to the piece of flesh Dolly had spit on the ground. His red face grew redder and he delivered more violent punches to Dolly's now bare midsection, causing her to vomit up the toast and coffee.

"I'm gonna fuck ya first, though," he whispered into Dolly's ear. "In the cunny first, to take that damned virginity, and then in your ass," he said with a chuckle, "because that's gonna make ya scream."

As he worked at the button on her skirt, Dolly screamed and struggled. "Get off me, Irish scum, get away."

He spun her back to face him and slapped Dolly again followed by another hard punch. "Settle down, darlin', I'm just gettin' started and when I'm done I think I'll walk you back to the wagon bound up just the way ya are as a little gift for Pauly." The bleeding Irishman grinned. "I'll make all the lasses watch while he administers his special brand of punishment as a warnin' not to misbehave."

The pain of the punches and the fear of what was coming caused Dolly to swoon. She fell into the sweet, painless darkness as the Irishman yanked down her skirt and ripped at her bloomers.

19

Trace had just passed the whore wagon when he heard a woman scream in the distance.

Knowing it could only be Dolly, Trace urged his horse into a gallop and strained his ears to hear more. He soon saw Dolly's gray mare in the road, loaded with items and Dolly suspended from the saddle with her arms above her head.

A man stood in front of her delivering slap after slap to her face and then began to punch Dolly in her exposed gut. Trace's blood boiled with rage at the man and guilt at himself. If he hadn't left her alone on the mountain, none of this would have happened to her.

As the man Trace recognized as the Irishman, took down his trousers and lifted Dolly's legs up around his waist, he took out his rifle and shot into the air. The man dropped Dolly's legs, scrambled to pull up his trousers and turned to face Trace.

"There's nothin' for ya to be concerned with here, Mister," the Irishman said as he took a kerchief from his pocket and put it to his bloody ear. "I run that wagon you just passed, and she be one of me lasses. We had a bit of a disagreement," he took the bloody kerchief and waved it, "and I was administerin' a bit of punishment."

Trace dismounted his horse and walked toward Dolly, who hung from Bess, unconscious. "I think she's had enough."

The Irishman grinned. "Not by a long shot. This girlie has a good deal to pay for." He pressed the kerchief to his ear again. "Would ya like to have a go at her yourself? She's prime and still—"

"Still what?" Trace asked with a tight grip on his rifle. Trace had a feeling he knew what the man was going to say.

"Let's just say she's still quite fresh and it would be an enjoyable poke for a fella like yourself. How 'bout I let ya have her here for free," the Irishman said and grinned as he twisted Dolly around and ran his hand over one of her smooth, firm ass cheeks. "You could even take your choice of holes to poke her in."

Trace's stomach heaved when the man spread the cheeks of Dolly's ass. "I find this hole quite pleasant," the Irishman said with the intent to entice.

"You're a disgusting piece of filth," Trace said before drawing back and slamming the butt of his riffle into the grinning man's mouth, sending him to the ground without several of his front teeth.

Trace dropped the rifle and went to his knees. He punched the man in the face several more times in his rage over what the man had done to Dolly. He outweighed the man by at least fifty pounds and all of that was muscle. The Irishman's face was now as bloody as his ear and disfigured by broken jaws on both sides of his head. Trace heard the man moan, choke, and then go silent.

Dolly moaned and attracted Trace's attention away from the silent pimp. He unwrapped the reins from around Dolly's arms and lowered her to the ground. With tears stinging his eyes, Trace lifted her head into his lap and brushed a gentle hand over her swelling face. "What did that bastard do to you?" he whispered as he ran his eyes over her naked bosom and down across her bruised belly. In shame, Trace stopped his eyes there. he tugged up her bloomers and skirt then rebuttoned her camisole and blouse. "You've been a busy girl while I was away," he said when he recognized the blouse fabric as one they'd purchased in Vernon.

As he finished straightening Dolly's clothes, he took stock of the items loaded upon the gray mare. He smiled. "It looks like you plan to be busier."

Trace lowered her head back to the ground and went to his horse for his canteen. He wet his kerchief and wiped Dolly's face To his relief, her swelling eyes fluttered open.

"Trace?" she said in a weak voice and reached up to touch his face with trembling fingers. "Is that really you or am I dreaming?"

Trace smiled down at her. "It's me, sweetheart and I'm so sorry for leaving you here all alone."

Dolly struggled up on her elbows and Trace helped her into a sitting position. She saw the Irishman in the ground and gasped. "Is he dead?"

"If he's not, he's gonna wish he was when he wakes up."

Dolly threw her arms around Trace's neck. "I love you, Trace," she mumbled into his shoulder, her voice so soft, Trace could hardly make out the words. "Please never leave me again."

"I love you too, Dolly," he replied sincerely, "and I won't."

They sat together holding one another until Dolly jerked her head off his shoulder and screamed. "Behind you, Trace!"

Trace released Dolly and reached for his rifle. He turned to see a burly, bearded man stalking toward them. He saw the Irishman on the ground and recognition bloomed on his face when he saw Dolly. "What did you do to Paddy and what are you doing with my redheaded whore?" He barreled toward them, reaching for Dolly. "She's ours and I intend to have her back, Mister."

Trace lifted the rifle. "Dolly doesn't belong to anybody," he yelled and fired at the charging man, "but me." Trace waited for the man to fall and then scooped Dolly into his arms. He held her while she wept, and he wept with her.

He'd killed three men for this woman. He didn't know how he felt about that and wondered how Dolly felt about it. Would she still see him as a good, god-fearing man or see him as a murderer? Dolly was alive and out of danger. That was all that mattered.

Dolly got to her feet. She stumbled over to the body of the bearded man, bent, and yanked a ring with an iron key on it hanging from his trousers. Then she walked to the Irishman, stared down at him for a few minutes, and kicked him in the head until his brains and blood oozed from his ears.

She turned to Trace with a stern look on her bruised face. "The bastard's dead now!"

Dolly walked to Bess and mounted with a few painful groans. She urged the horse down the trail and Trace followed. At the wagon, three men sat waiting around the fire. "This wagon's closed for business, fellas," she hissed. "You'd best be on your way."

One of the men stood, followed by the others. "We've been waiting for a bit of cunny for a while now. That man said he'd be right back."

"Yah," one of the others said, "we done paid." He narrowed his eyes and took a step toward Dolly. "Your cunny will do. Don't ya think, fellas"

Trace fired his rifle into the air. "You'd be smart to do as the lady said and be on your way back to your camp."

The men ran back to the trail and disappeared toward the logging operation.

Dolly took the key and opened the iron door at the back of the wagon. The aroma of unwashed women and an overfilled chamber pot wafted out, causing Trace to cover his nose and gag.

One of the older women stood and stepped to the door. "Where are Paddy and Paul?"

"Dead," Dolly said bluntly.

"What about us?" the woman asked with her eyes wide.

"You're free," Dolly said and tossed the woman the key. "Do you know how to hitch that horse to the wagon and drive it?"

The woman nodded as she unlocked her shackle and then passed the keys along to the next woman. "We all had to take turns hitching and unhitching Clyde," she said, "but we can't exactly go drivin' down the road like this." She motioned to her naked body.

Dolly began removing her blouse and skirt. She handed them to the woman. "Put these on and follow this trail into the little town ahead. It's about two hours. Go to Sanders' Mercantile and tell the woman what's happened to you." Dolly studied the woman. "The bodies of those men are just a little way up the trail. I reckon the money they've been paid for your services is on one or the both of them. Take it and ask Mrs. Sanders to fit all of you with new clothes from her store."

The other women crowded to the door wide-eyed. "You mean we don't have to do this anymore and can go home if we want to?" a very young girl asked with tears in her big brown eyes.

"You're free to go wherever and do whatever you please," Dolly told her, standing in her camisole, bloomers, and boots. She pointed toward the north. "I think there's a creek just through those trees if you all want to wash up some.

Trace didn't think he could be more proud. He turned his horse back toward the trail and looked away as naked women jumped out of the wagon and hugged Dolly for giving them their freedom.

Trace knew most, if not all of them, would never be welcomed back into their homes again, if they ever had one. They were whores now and would likely finish their lives as whores in one place or another. Hopefully it wouldn't be in a filthy wagon like that one with men like Davis, the Irishman, and his henchman.

Dolly mounted Bess and joined Trace on the trail. They hurried past the Snydergaard place when they came to it. Neither of them wanted the old couple to see Dolly riding in her underthings.

"What is all of this?" Trace finally asked, nodding to the bolts of cloth and bundles tied to poor Bess.

"Supplies," Dolly said with a grin. "Please don't make me laugh. It really hurts. I promise to explain it all tomorrow."

"I'm gonna hold you to it."

"That was a pretty blouse and right useful lookin' skirt," Trace told her. "I'm sorry you had to lose them."

Dolly shook her head. "It's all right. I don't think I could have worn them again anyhow after what happened today."

"It was all my fault, Dolly. I shouldn't have left you alone with the need to go into Vernon. I'm so sorry."

"The decision to go into town was mine, Trace. I really didn't need to, but I wanted to," she said with a sigh. "I needed to test my independence."

"Do you want to be independent, Dolly?" Trace asked with worry nagging at him. Had he driven her away?

Dolly took a deep breath. "I don't want to live my life as somebody's house slave anymore and I don't want to live my life as somebody's whore either."

Trace grinned over at her in the fading light. "Isn't that what a wife is?" He chuckled. "A house slave and somebody's personal whore?"

"I don't know, Trace" she said, returning his grin. "Does a wife get a dollar every time she lets her husband give her a poke?"

Trace broke out into boisterous laughter. "You've got me there with that, Dolly." His laughter quieted as they neared the cabin. "Lucy asked me that same question once." He stared at the cabin, remembering the pretty blonde who'd shared his bed for nearly ten years. "She had a gallon jar almost full of silver dollars beside the bed when she died."

"What's all of this?" Dolly asked when she saw the wagon in front of the house.

Trace smiled. "My past," he said with a sigh, "and our future."

20

Dolly stood behind Vivian Sanders, tying a lace-trimmed bow over the bustled skirt of the dress she'd carefully sewn for the woman.

"It's absolutely gorgeous," Vivian gushed as she stared at her reflection in the full-length oval mirror standing in her bedroom.

"Bend down for a minute," Dolly told the woman and when she did, Dolly pinned something to her head. "I made this little bonnet. It's not exactly like the one in the picture, but it's close."

Vivian lifted her head and stared at her reflection. Her hand went to the bonnet made from the same fabric as the dress and trimmed with lace and ribbon. Dolly saw tears coming to Vivian's eyes as she gasped, "It's absolutely divine," and wrapped her arms around Dolly. "You're a miracle worker, Madame Dolly and I can't wait to show this off at the dance on Saturday." Vivian hugged her again. "Every woman on the mountain is going to want you to make them one." Vivian grinned. "But not like this one. I want this one to be all my own."

"I promise to keep this pattern just for you," Dolly told her then she grinned. "Though I might want to make one something like it for myself for a special occasion."

Dolly had to guess at the size because she'd forgotten the piece of paper with Vivian's measurements was still in her skirt when she'd given it to the woman in the wagon, but the dress fit perfectly and looked very much like the color plate in the fashion periodical.

"You could make one like it in white for a wedding dress," Vivian chirped. "I'd even order the satin for you as my gift if you'd like and display it here in the store."

"That's sweet of you, Vivian, but white satin isn't very practical for the wife of a mountain man." She glanced at Trace. "If anything, I've found that the mountain people up here are very practical."

"I got some lovely polished cotton in, then. There is some beautiful mint green and lavender that would look gorgeous with that red hair of your."

Dolly smiled. "Let's go have a look at it."

When they returned to the cabin that night, Dolly had made them some toasted bread. Trace sliced off some ham and she warmed it, along with the bread. As they ate ham between slices of bread, slathered with Dolly's sweet plum butter, Trace had taken her hand, sank to his knees and asked her to be his wife.

"A real wife with words spoken before a minister in church?" Dolly asked uneasily.

"It's only fair," he told her. "I married Lucy in a church before all her kin. Why should I expect any different for you?"

"Dolly wrapped her sore arms around his neck and kissed Trace like she'd never kissed him before. "I love you, Trace Anderson. I've loved you for years."

"And I love you, Dolly Stroud," Trace said and kissed her again. "I swear I'll love you for all the years left in my life."

He hugged her until he heard her grown in pain. Trace let her go and stepped back. "I'm so sorry." He glanced into the parlor at all the fabric piled on the chairs. "Now will you tell what's going on with all of that?"

Dolly took a deep breath and smiled. "I'm an independent businesswoman now," she said, squaring her shoulders in the chair as she went on to tell Trace about her arrangement with Vivian

Sanders. "She wants to carry your leather goods in the mercantile too."

"Are you going to be my business manager, Mrs. Anderson?"

"Maybe if you build me some shelves to store my fabric on and a bigger table for cutting on, Mr. Anderson."

Trace grinned. "There's a big table I use in my shop out there on that wagon and you're welcome to use it. There will be plenty of shelves in the shop I plan to build with Fredrick, as well." Trace pointed to the wall where the wardrobe stood. "I suppose we'll have to share it."

Dolly kissed him. "I'll share everything with you, Trace."

Trace rolled his eyes. "We'll see how that works out when you need to cut material for a dress someone ordered, and I need to cut leather for something."

"We'll make it work," she said with a yawn.

"You've had a rough day," he said and stood. "I'll see you in the morning."

Dolly clutched at his hand. "Don't leave me, please."

Trace glanced at the bed. "Are you sure that's what you want?"

"I know I don't want to be alone anymore and I don't want you sleeping in the stable." Dolly squeezed his hand. "Please stay here with me." She pulled Trace to her and kissed him again. "I love you, Trace and I want you to stay with me."

Trace touched her face. "I'll stay in here with you, but not in the bed. I'll put my bedroll on the floor in the parlor until we're hitched proper by a minister." He smiled. "When do you want to do it?"

"Vivian Sanders wants her dress for the Summer Dance in three weeks can you wait until after that?"

"And after you make a dress for yourself," he said with a kiss on her forehead. "I'll go out and get my bedroll."

Trace left the house and Dolly went to the wardrobe where she took out her night dress and dressing gown, slipped out of her underthings and covered up with her night clothes.

Over the next three weeks, Dolly and Trace's life was a flurry of activity. Dolly went to the plum thicket and filled a peck basket with the fat, red plums for Helga and Fredrick. Trace and the old man staked out the corners for the shop space and a large bedroom.

Trace brought the furniture from the house in Concho into the cabin. Dolly did her best to arrange it all and still be able to have room to walk through the room. Trace stored the things from his shop in the stable except for the large table which he left in front of the house, near the porch.

Dolly used it to spread the fabric for Vivian's dress upon, sketch out the pattern in chalk and cut it out. She took her time and cut carefully. She did the same with the sewing, making certain every seam was straight and double tacked in places that might be stressed like beneath the arms and at the waist. Dolly took her time hemming the delicate lace before she ruffled it and used satin ribbon to tack down the lace edges. It took Dolly almost the entire three weeks to finish the dress, apron, and bonnet.

"It's real pretty, Dolly," Trace told her as he studied her seams. "You do very good work and should be proud."

Dolly's face flushed with embarrassment as hammering began. Fredrick and his son-in-law had begun framing the new additions. "Thank you, Trace. I can't wait to make shirts for you. I just need to take your measurements first. You're a lot bigger than Martin." She giggled. "This hammering is going to drive me and my poor chickens mad though."

The mention of Martin's name made Trace's skin crawl. As far as he was concerned, Martin Stroud deserved to be in a grave beside Davis, the sheriff, and the other two men Trace had killed. He was damned lucky he hadn't been strangled in the street that day.

"Let's not talk about your worthless brother, Dolly. This is our time now. We are beginning a new life together and don't need him in it."

"He's my brother, Trace, and the only family I have left. We should at least invite him to the wedding." Dolly shrugged. "We can invite him and if he doesn't want to come, he doesn't have to."

Trace didn't want people to know where he and Dolly were. He still worried about them finding the sheriff's grave.

Trace released a long sigh. "He doesn't give a good goddamn about you, Dolly. He sold you to Davis without a bit of thought about what that bastard intended for you. All he cared about was that his debts had been covered."

"At least the house is paid off again and without me there to hold him back, Martin can get on with his life."

Mr. Evans at the bank told me Martin has already remortgaged the house, Dolly. He's strutting around town in fancy new clothes and saying you're gonna be back any day when everyone knows you went off to San Francisco with Davis."

Dolly's mouth dropped open and tears filled her eyes. "Is that what they're saying about me at home—that I'm a whore?"

Trace took her into his arms and kissed the top of her head. "This is your home now, Dolly and all I'm calling you is my wife. Shall we take that beautiful dress into town for Vivian to try on?"

Dolly swiped the tears from her face and forced a smile. "Yes, let's."

They made the long trip into town with the dress folded and wrapped in paper Dolly had saved. They walked into the mercantile and Vivian greeted them with water.

"Is that my dress?" she asked with glee as she took the package from Dolly and hugged it to her chest. "Oh, I can't wait to see it and then wear it to the Dance."

Trace smiled and handed her his empty cup. "And then you can wear it to our wedding."

Vivian's mouth went agape. "But I thought you were already married."

Trace glanced at Dolly with his face going pale. "It was only a civil ceremony before," he said, recovering, "but now we want to do it right in church before a minister."

Vivian smiled. "Well, of course you do. When is the happy occasion?"

Trace shrugged. "That's just it. I've got to find a minister and a church."

"Reverend Porter comes through on his circuit every few weeks and holds services in the Town Hall. I'm certain he'll be at the

Dance, Saturday night." Vivian smiled. "Shall I make arrangements with him for the ceremony in the Hall the next time he's in Vernon?"

Trace took Dolly's hand. "That sounds good to us."

Vivian beamed as she held the package. "Let's go try this on," she said with a girlish giggle and took Dolly's hand to lead her up to the apartment.

They traveled home that afternoon with the makings of Dolly's wedding dress and Vivian's promise to send her son to the cabin with word of the date the Reverend would be in town next, along with the building supplies Trace had ordered.

As they were leaving, Vivian took Dolly's arm. "Thank you for sending that wag … eh … those poor women my way."

Dolly had wondered if Vivian would mention the wagon filled with unclad women. "I hope they were no trouble, ma'am."

Vivian rolled her eyes and whispered, "Damned near cleaned me out of every ready to wear, woman's garments, blankets, and a good bit of the food stuffs I had in the store." She raised a brow. "I worried some they wouldn't be able to pay, but that gal in your clothes had a sack full of coins and it made my month."

"Did they say where they were going?" Dolly asked as Trace tied their packages on the horses.

"I think two of them took rooms in the saloon," she said, "and the gal in your clothes said she was taking the wagon on in to Show Low in hopes of selling it for money to send some of the others out on Butterfields."

"That's good," Dolly said. "I'm glad they were no trouble to you."

Vivian smiled. "You can send trouble like that to my door any day," she said, patting her cash box.

As they rode home, Trace gave her some news. "I sent a telegram down to Herman Evans at the bank while you and Vivian were doing your primping."

"And?" she said, adjusting her sore bottom in the saddle. She hadn't had a chance to make a new split skirt yet and her bare thighs were beginning to sting.

"He sold the house," Trace told her with a sad smile. "I told him to wire the funds from the sale to the bank in Show Low where I keep an account."

"How much did he get for it?"

Trace smiled. "Three hundred," he said, "because I left so much furniture behind in it."

"You seem a little sad about that."

"It's hard to think of somebody else sleepin' in me and Lucy's bed,"

"You could have brought it for you and me to sleep in," Dolly said with a sheepish grin.

Trace rolled his eyes. "I think that would have been harder." He smiled across at her as he patted his horse's neck. "Anyhow, I don't think the poor horses could have hauled anymore weight up the mountain. That wagon was loaded."

"And I don't know where we'd have put another bed," Dolly said with a giggle.

When they arrived home, they found the cabin had practically doubled in size. Fredrick and his son-in-law had completely enclosed the new shop area as well as the space for the new bedroom. Inside, they'd removed the window at the foot of the bed and cut a door into the bedroom and drilled holes into the log wall to begin cutting a door into the shop area.

Dolly peeked into the dark space to be the bedroom and sighed. "This is huge. There will be plenty of room for the bed, wardrobe and washbasin in here."

Trace kissed her cheek. "And maybe a crib someday?"

Dolly felt her cheeks flush. "Maybe."

Dolly knew Trace wanted a child and so did she, but the memory of Lucy's death in childbed worried her. Dolly was built larger than Lucy had been, but she'd known women her size and larger who'd died giving birth. Death in childbed was a common fear amongst women, but she knew even more women who'd gone through it and survived. Many had gone through it several times.

Dolly stepped back into the light and smiled. "I'll give you as many children as I can."

He kissed her cheek. "I'm lookin' forward to all the tryin'."

She slapped his shoulder playfully and went to the stove to fry up some of Fredrick's spicy sausages and potatoes with chopped onions for their supper. While the potatoes cooked, she warmed some cornbread.

"You're truly amazin', Dolly," Trace said as he sat down to the meal Dolly set out on the china he'd brought up from Concho.

The china hutch now sat against the wall between the stove and the bed. Dolly intended to move it to the spot where the bed now stood after the bedroom had been completed. She gazed around the cabin. Everything would be so different in a matter of weeks. Trace's hunting cabin would be a house, that house would be their home, and Dolly would be a married woman.

"Thank you, Trace," she said, "for everything."

21

More rain arrived the following day, bringing outdoor activities to a halt.

Trace, with Dolly's help, managed to get the big table inside the new shop area and she began cutting the fabric for her wedding dress. She adjusted the pattern pieces she'd made for Vivian's dress to fit herself. Dolly had all the pieces cut out in just a little over an hour while Trace sawed through the logs and chinking for the new door into the house.

Though the dress was a priority, Dolly couldn't ignore her household duties and before the rain set in too hard, she fed the chickens and picked a basket full of beans to can. She sat in the chair on the porch to snap the crisp, green beans as the rain came down through the boughs, filling the air with the fresh, clean scent of pine. Dolly looked forward to decorating the house for Christmas and hoped she'd be with child by then, though it would only be a few months after their wedding.

That evening a dozen quart jars of green beans sat on the counter ready to go onto the shelves in the cellar. Seeing them gave Dolly a proud sense of accomplishment, as did the supper she fixed of pork chops, green beans seasoned with bacon, and fresh hot biscuits.

Trace had sawed through the logs on one side of the opening and came to the table exhausted.

"Who'd have thought cutting a three foot door would be so hard," he said working the tightness from his shoulder. "I'm gonna need some horse liniment on this before I go to bed tonight."

"I've got some cream Helga made that she swears is good for muscle pains." Dolly smiled. "And it's made for humans not horses."

"I'm told I'm as big as a horse," Trace said, as he bit into a pork chop, "so I reckon horse medicine would work on me just as well."

Dolly laughed as she filled her plate. "Well, let's try the medicine made for humans before we use up that made for the horses."

"I'll leave that to you then, Mrs. Anderson." He glanced at the jars on the counter. "Those'll be good eatin' this winter."

"I'm going to let the pole beans dry," she said, "and shell them."

"Boiled beans with ham will make a damned good meal along with your sweet cornbread."

"There's not much left of that pig hanging out there," Dolly said and held up a chop.

"Fredrick's butcherin' a steer next week and bringin' us half of it for the smoke house," Trace said with a smile. "How do beef roasts and steaks sound for a change?"

"When the carrots are big enough to pull, I want a big pot of beef stew," Dolly said with a sigh.

After washing up the dishes, Dolly went to Trace where he sprawled on his pallet on the parlor floor and rubbed the aromatic cream Helga had given her on his bare shoulders. He sighed as the minty ingredients began to warm his aching muscles. Dolly felt a thrill run through her body as she ran her hands over Trace's hard rippling muscles, pressing and kneading them harder when he moaned with pleasure.

She couldn't wait to be this man's wife and have him lie next to her at night and …" Dolly squeezed her eyes shut. She still didn't know if she was going to be able to bear him touching her in intimate places after the attack by the Irishman. She still had nightmares about Davis's cock being shoved into her mouth and the searing pain of the sheriff in her behind. Would Trace want to do those things to her? Dolly didn't know if she could bear it.

The day of the wedding approached, and Dolly's nerves had begun to fray. She'd finished the dress in a week and even made Trace a shirt from the soft green fabric she'd made the apron from. The green accented the lavender beautifully and she couldn't wait to wear her creation for everyone to see.

Dolly needed to get out into the fresh air away from the cramped cabin and the hammering of cedar shingles being put on the roof, so she picked up her basket and headed for the blackberry patch where she'd seen fat, ripe berries the other day when she'd ventured down to the creek for fresh greens.

The sun was bright in the clear, blue sky and Dolly was glad for her bonnet. She didn't want to show up at her wedding with a sunburned nose. A blue jay squawked at Dolly as she passed below her nest. She made her way into the patch of thorny canes and began filling her basket. Unable to resist, Dolly popped a fat, sweet berry into her mouth and chewed. She sighed with delight as the juice filled her mouth and she vowed to bake a cobbler for Trace tonight.

As Dolly picked her way through the thorny patch she heard the ominous rattle of a snake and halted. Getting a snake bite would certainly put off the wedding. Clutching the near full basket to her chest and with her heart thudding in her chest, Dolly backed her way out of the patch of berries the way she'd come and hurried back to the cabin.

"Where have you been?" Trace called down to her from the roof of the back porch he'd added between the bedroom and shop additions. It's where she'd do her washing now.

Dolly lifted the basket. "Picking berries for a cobbler."

Trace smiled and patted his belly. "You're too good to me, woman."

Dolly noted the crates delivered from Sanders' Mercantile Trace had told her were wedding presents and couldn't be opened until they returned. "And you're too good to me, my love," she called back and slipped into the empty shop and then the house.

The scents of fried bacon and coffee lingered from breakfast as Dolly dumped her basket of berries into the washtub to clean and stem. While they soaked, Dolly cut butter into a bowl of flour to make dough for the flakey crust. With more berries than her pie tin would hold, Dolly rolled out the dough and pressed it into a deep skillet poured in the fresh berries, covered them with sugar, a little butter, and then covered it all with the other dough and pinched the edges together. Dolly brushed the top with a beaten egg and sprinkled the unbaked crust with a little sugar before sliding the heavy skillet into the oven.

The rest of the afternoon Dolly spent making Trace's supper of fried chicken. He'd slaughtered one of the young roosters that morning. Dolly had plucked, gutted it, and now cut the bird into pieces to flour and fry. Mashed young potatoes, green peas in the pods, gravy, and biscuits rounded out the meal.

Dolly called Trace in to supper and stared around the cabin. It smelled of fried chicken and cobbler and Dolly knew she was going to be happy here—happier than she'd ever dreamed she could be when she'd lived with Martin and happier than she'd ever imagined she'd be after that horrid day in her bedroom with Davis. Davis had made her a whore that day but Trace still wanted to make her his wife.

Tears of gratitude, love, and joy stung her eyes as Trace came in the door and Dolly threw herself into his arms. "I love you, Trace," Dolly said into his broad, sweaty chest, choking back her tears.

"I love you too, babe," he said and kissed the top of her head, "but let's eat. I'm starved. My belly thinks my throat's been cut."

Dolly smiled as she watched her man go to the table. Yes, she was going to be very happy here as Mrs. Dolly Anderson.

On the morning of the wedding, Dolly washed her hair and combed it out to dry on the way into Vernon. They were taking the wagon, so Dolly dressed in the green calico dress rather than a riding skirt. Her wedding dress was carefully folded and wrapped in paper for the trip. She would change into it at Vivian's and then walk to the Town Hall. Fredrick had agreed to walk her down the aisle and stand with Trace as his best man. Vivian would stand with Dolly as her maid of honor.

"All right," Vivian said with a pout as she stared at Dolly in her wedding dress, "now I'm envious. This dress is so much prettier than mine."

Dolly stared at her reflection in the mirror. the lavender gown was trimmed with mint-green ribbon along the lace at the collar and three-quarter sleeves while the mint-green apron was trimmed with lavender ribbon above the ruffled white lace she'd trimmed it with. She felt like a princess in a storybook as she twirled in front of the mirror.

"Let's put this on," Vivian said as she pinned a white lace veil on Dolly's red hair she'd masterfully pinned atop the young woman's head. Vivian smiled when she handed Dolly a bouquet of pale purple Irises peppered with sprigs of white Lily of the Valley.

Dolly put the flowers to her nose and inhaled the sweet scents. "Thank you, Vivian. They're perfect."

"I think you're ready to go become Mrs. Anderson before the congregation." Vivian, wearing the dress Dolly had made for her, put her arm through Dolly's and walked with her down from the apartment and through the mercantile.

At the door to the Hall, Vivian gave Dolly's arm to Fredrick and with her own bouquet in hand motioned for the pianist to begin playing the Wedding March. To the oows and ahhs of the people assembled in the room, Fredrick walked Dolly down the aisle to stand beside Trace, who wore a black suit and the soft green shirt she'd made for him. Dolly had never seen a more handsome man.

Trace had just slipped a narrow gold band upon her finger and the minister introduced them as Mr. and Mrs. Trace Anderson when the door into the Hall burst open. "It's time to come back home where you belong, Dolly Stroud," her brother Martin yelled and from his slurred speech, Dolly could tell he'd been drinking heavily.

He stumbled up the aisle in his dirty suit and dented bowler hat and grabbed Dolly's arm away from Trace. "Come on Dolly," he demanded as he pulled on her arm. "it's time you quit playing the whore in this thieving bastard's bed and came home with me." Martin laughed. "The house needs cleaning and I oughta beat your ass for leaving me the way you did to whore with him."

Dolly's mouth fell open and her cheeks turned scarlet as she heard the murmuring in the crowd. Trace came forward and shoved Martin. "Who the hell are you callin' a thief, Martin." Trace scowled at his new brother-in-law.

"I'm calling you a thief, Anderson because you stole my sister without paying my bride-price." Martin pointed a finger at Trace "And you've turned her into your damned whore."

Trace drew back his arm and landed a punch on Martin's mouth. "I just married her, Martin," Trace hissed. "Dolly's my wife now and no longer your personal house servant to order around and beat like a damned dog."

Martin stumbled back to his feet and pointed his finger at Trace. "She's my property, Anderson, to do with as I please until you've paid my bride-price of a hundred dollars."

Dolly stormed past the wedding party that stood wide-eyed with their mouths agape and slapped her brother's stubbled cheek. "You've already been paid Martin," she said in a voice only he could hear, "and I'm nobody's property— not your's, not his, and certainly not a man called Davis's. Now get out!" Dolly yelled. "You weren't invited, Martin, and you're not wanted here."

Trace took Dolly's arm in his as he grinned at the pitiful Martin Stroud, who'd finally been put in his place by his sister. "You heard my wife, Martin," Trace bellowed before the awestruck crowd. "Get the hell out before I boot your drunken ass out."

"I need you to come back home, Dolly," Martin mumbled as he stumbled down the aisle toward the door. "You owe me, bitch," he said, turning to make one last slur before Trace took a step toward him and he fled.

Trace took Dolly's hand again. "We're sorry for the interruption, folks," he said with a grin, "but you know how in-laws can be."

The crowd laughed, and the Reverend cleared his throat for attention. "Would you care to kiss your bride, Mr. Anderson?"

Trace smiled down at Dolly and lifted her veil and stared into her sparkling blue eyes. "Indeed I would."

EPILOGUE

Christmas arrived on the mountain with snow. Dolly had decorated the house with pine boughs, pinecones, and red velvet ribbons. She didn't have a fireplace, but Trace had divided the parlor and the kitchen with a wall and built her a sturdy, mantle-like shelf which Dolly hung stockings from. She decorated a small tree in the corner with iced cookies, peppermint canes Helga had made for her, and garlands of the red ribbon. At the very top, Trace crowned the tree with a star he'd cut from a piece of shiny metal. Dolly thought it couldn't have been more perfect.

They shared a Christmas Dinner of roast and stuffed goose, baked yams, a Norwegian bread stuffed with candied fruit and nuts, and a rich plum pudding with Fredrick and Helga in their farmhouse. Dolly contributed green beans and a blackberry/raspberry pie topped with whipped sweetened cream. They exchanged gifts of handmade goods and toasted with cups of rich eggnog—something Dolly had never tasted.

Upon finishing and supplying his shop with raw leather, Trace had gone to work and supplied the mercantile in Vernon with every sort of leather good. Through Fredrick's son-in-law, he'd made connections with lumbermen and he had orders for several custom harnesses and straps for climbing and cutting limbs in the high canopy.

The popularity of Vivian's dress and Dolly's wedding dress brought the new bride a flurry of orders from women on the mountain. Her bolts of fabric took up almost as much shelf space in the shop as Trace's leather. Her fingers were raw from all the sewing she'd done to finish Christmas orders. Vivian had also enlarged her ready-to-wear section in the mercantile and made Dolly her supplier. Trace and Dolly were active members of the community and considered pillars of business.

They sat side-by-side on the settee in the parlor sipping coffee after their day with Fredrick and Helga. "I have a present for you, Mrs. Anderson," Trace said and jumped up to rush off to the shop. He came back carrying something on a black iron stand. "Where do you think we should put this?" he asked, as he pulled off the cloth.

Dolly's mouth fell open as she stared at the sewing machine. It was one she'd pointed out to Trace in one of her periodicals and mentioned how handy one would be.

"Oh, my gracious," she said with her hand at her mouth. "When did you get this?"

He grinned. "I picked it up in Show Low while you were out making your deliveries last week."

Trace had done everything he could think of to make Dolly's life easier. His wedding presents to her had been washtubs with wringers like the one's she'd bought in Concho and an upholstered commode chair for the bedroom, so she needn't squat over a chamber pot any longer.

Dolly wrapped her arms around her husband's neck and kissed him. "I have something for you too," she said, with an impish grin.

"Well, what is it?" he asked, when she didn't move away.

"I haven't needed my clouts since the month we married," Dolly said.

After waiting a few minutes for him to reason out what his wife was saying, Trace's hazel eyes went wide "You mean you're —"

Dolly smiled and put her hand to her abdomen. "By my reckoning, about planting time this spring, I'll be delivering a harvest of my own."

Trace swept Dolly up in his arms and swung her around with a loud whoop. He glanced down at the new sewing machine. "I guess that thing is really going to come in handy now with all the baby things you're gonna need to make."

Dolly rolled her eyes. "And maternity clothes."

They kissed again before returning to their seats on the settee. "Merry Christmas, Mr. Anderson," Dolly whispered in his ear.

"It certainly has been, Mrs. Anderson. You couldn't have given me a better gift."

Dear reader,

We hope you enjoyed reading *Dolly*. Please take a moment to leave a review in Amazon, even if it's a short one. Your opinion is important to us.

Discover more books by Lori Beasley Bradley at https://www.nextchapter.pub/authors/lori-beasley-bradley

Want to know when one of our books is free or discounted for Kindle? Join the newsletter at http://eepurl.com/bqqB3H

Best regards,

Lori Beasley Bradley and the Next Chapter Team

ACKNOWLEDGMENTS

I'd like to thank you for reading Dolly. If you liked the book, please go to Amazon.com and leave a review and tell me what you liked about it. If you didn't like it, please go there and tell me why you didn't and how I can improve.

Thank you to my Content Editor Daniel Holmes. You always give me great constructive criticism and I appreciate it.

Thank you to Angela Rydell for your valuable assistance with this manuscript.

You might also like:

Dreams of Molly by Lori Beasley Bradley

To read the first chapter for free go to:
https://www.nextchapter.pub/books/dreams-of-molly